"Reading opens new doors to the world"

This
Book was
generously
donated to the
St. Margaret
Middle School Library
by

The Sabatino
Family,
2003

Italian Fairy Tales

Italian fairy tales number among the most charming of all and are, as well, of great interest. They combine elements from both the East and the West, incorporating details from the Arabian Nights with a dash of Celtic symbolism. Some even reflect a Japanese influence. At the same time they are characteristically Italian, full of sunshine and humour, reflecting the Italian temperament and almost entirely lacking in really villainous villains. Many of the legends which have become most famous throughout the world, such as Cinderella, Beauty and the Beast, and Puss in Boots, were first told in Italy.

Miss Lum, who has travelled extensively in many countries throughout the world, here retells some of the most enchanting of these old stories, which will delight the regular readers of our Fairy Tale series and win many new ones to their ranks.

The World Fairy Tale Collections

BURMESE AND THAI FAIRY TALES	*Eleanor Brockett*
DANISH FAIRY TALES	*Inge Hack*
FAIRY TALES FROM SWEDEN	*Irma Kaplan*
ITALIAN FAIRY TALES	*Peter Lum*
JAPANESE FAIRY TALES	*Juliet Piggott*
PORTUGUESE FAIRY TALES	*Maurice and Pamela Michael*

To be published

NORWEGIAN FAIRY TALES	*Gert Strindberg*
PERSIAN FAIRY TALES	*Eleanor Brockett*
TURKISH FAIRY TALES	*Eleanor Brockett*

Italian Fairy Tales

Retold by
PETER LUM

Illustrated by Harry and Ilse Toothill

FOLLETT PUBLISHING COMPANY
CHICAGO NEW YORK

First published 1963 by Frederick Muller Ltd., London, England.

Published 1967 in the United States of America by Follett Publishing Company. *Manufactured in the United States of America.*

Library of Congress Catalog Card Number: 67-21171

FIRST PRINTING

Follett Publishing Company
1010 West Washington Boulevard
Chicago, Illinois 60607

T/L 4395

Contents

Illustrations

Introduction

ITALY AS A nation, politically united, is a very new country. It was only in 1861, a hundred years ago, that the Kingdom of Piedmont won control over the entire country and the Kingdom of Italy came into existence. Before that time the land had been divided into separate Kingdoms, Dukedoms, Papal States (those which were ruled by the Pope), Republics and City States. There were Tuscany and Lombardy, Piedmont and Savoy, and Sicily; Rome and Venice, Florence and Naples and Milan; but there was no single nation of Italy.

Yet Italy, geographically, is one of the most definite countries in the world. It is a peninsula, surrounded on three sides by the sea, and cut off from the rest of Europe on the fourth side by the Alps. The Italian people, whatever their governments might be, have long been one people.

The fairy tales which the Italians tell are, therefore, usually well known from one end of the country to the other. The name of the hero changes, and the details of his adventures, but the same story will appear in the north and the south, the east and the west. The story-telling Parrot, for instance, is best known in Tuscany and in Sicily, far apart though these two districts are. The adventures of Giufà, with numerous variations, and changing names, are told throughout Italy. So are the stories which tell how Beppo Pipetta, or Padre Ulivo, or whoever it may be, outwitted Death and the Devil and argued his way into Heaven.

There are local variations, especially in the south. In the south and south-east, they still remember the Moorish or Saracen raiders who occupied and plundered the whole southern tip of the peninsula during the ninth century, capturing the ports of Bari and Brindisi and even threatening Rome. The villain of a story there is always dark. In fact, that may be why in Italian fairy tales to be fair-skinned is to be beautiful; to be dark is to be ugly.

In the great seaports such as Venice and Genoa tales are naturally told of the sea, of trade with foreign lands. Some of the stories themselves were imported from other lands, and are very like stories told in India or in China, as well as in France and other parts of Europe. Along the coasts of Italy, or on the islands, the stories are of fishermen and sailors. In the rich farming country of northern Italy they are of farmers, landlords and peasants.

Everywhere the influence of Christianity is felt, even in tales which echo a time before Christ. Christ Himself and His disciples often appear in the stories in a most informal way. Churches are not dim, silent places to be visited on Sunday, but a part of people's life, a place to drop in any time for a prayer, or a gossip, or just to get warm.

Perhaps for this reason the only true villain, the only really evil character in Italian fairy tales, is the Devil. Every other person has redeeming features. Others may be foolish, or mistaken, or greedy, or selfish, but in the end they see the error of their ways and reform. Witches are good-hearted; giants, who love human flesh, are quite willing to eat macaroni instead. Even Cinderella's sisters in the story as it is told in Italy, where it originated, are not wicked. Only the Devil remains evil. He must, being the Devil. And he, fortunately, is so stupid that almost any sensible human being can outwit him.

These tales when they are told in Italy usually begin with the traditional 'There was a time,' or 'Once upon a time'. But they end a little differently from stories told in other lands. Instead of saying 'They lived happily ever after,' the teller is more likely to say – 'So *they* are happy and contented, and here we are without anything,' or sometimes – 'And here we are, picking our teeth.'

The story-teller is also quite likely to end up by saying – 'Now you must tell me your story, for mine is told.'

So let us begin. 'Once upon a time . . .'

ONE

Beppo Pipetta and his Knapsack

ONCE UPON A time a brave but reckless young soldier whose name was Beppo Pipetta happened to be passing through a lonely forest when he came upon a man, dressed like a well-to-do merchant, who was being attacked by two robbers. Beppo liked nothing better than a fight, and he immediately fell upon the robbers with such force that they soon fled for their lives. Then, seeing that the merchant was apparently unharmed, he went about his own business without even waiting for the man to say thank you.

Beppo had no idea that the man he had rescued was in fact the King, who often disguised himself in this way when he wanted to travel about his kingdom unattended. But the grateful ruler, having found out who his benefactor was, lost no time in summoning Beppo to the palace to receive a reward. There he announced that Beppo need no longer serve as a soldier unless he wanted to. He was free to go where he liked, do as he pleased, and the King would support him as long as he lived.

Beppo was delighted at this turn of events. He had no liking for work, and was quite happy to spend the rest of his life enjoying himself without having to worry about making a living. He threw away his knapsack and went off to his own village to visit his relations and tell them the good news. There one day, soon after he had reached home, he met a stranger in the street and after they had chatted away for some time they went into an inn together to have supper. The ex-soldier was still wearing his uniform, and as they sat down the stranger said to him:

'Why, if you are a soldier, do you not carry a knapsack?'

'I threw it away,' said Beppo. 'I did not like to be burdened. Anyway, I can do as I like from now on. I have a kind master who supports me and pays all my bills for me.'

'I see,' said the other man. 'You are very lucky. All the same, I have a knapsack here that I would like to give you.'

'What do I want with another knapsack when I have just got rid of my own?'

'I think you will find this one more valuable than your old one.' The stranger picked up his knapsack, which was a very large one, and placed it on the table between them. 'If you open this up and simply say – "Jump in!" – whoever you are talking to will find that, try as he may to avoid it, he must jump straight into the knapsack, and will never be able to get out again until you give permission.'

'If that is so,' said Beppo, who was by no means stupid, 'why are you giving it away?'

'I have enjoyed it long enough, and grown tired of its tricks.'

So saying, the stranger went on his way and left Beppo staring after him. 'Well,' the young soldier thought to himself, 'I might as well find out whether this knapsack really will do what he says it will. If it does it will certainly be worth keeping.'

At that moment the innkeeper came up to the table with his bill.

'What do you want?' asked Beppo.

'What do you think I want?' retorted the landlord. 'I want my bill paid.'

Beppo opened the mouth of the knapsack. 'Jump in,' he said, and to his surprise the landlord immediately leapt across the table in front of him and disappeared into the sack.

'Well, well,' Beppo murmured quietly to himself. 'It does work.' Then he laughed and said in a loud voice, which the landlord could easily hear: 'You see, my dear man, I am not the ordinary sort of fellow whom you should expect to pay your bills. Now if I promise to let you out I am sure that you will agree to forget all about the bill?'

'You rogue!' shouted the innkeeper indignantly from inside the sack; 'I will do nothing of the kind. Let me out of here at once!'

He went on protesting and struggling for quite a long time, while Beppo said nothing. But when he finally realized that all his efforts were in vain and that there was nothing whatever he could do to get himself out of the sack, he promised that if Beppo would only release him he would never again ask for the bill to be paid. Then Beppo let him out and, taking up the knapsack, went on his way.

Before long he came to another inn, and went in to refresh himself. There he fell into conversation with another man, and when it came time to pay the bill this man proudly brought out a magic purse and explained to Beppo that the purse always remained full of money, no matter how much money anyone took out of it.

'That must be very useful,' said Beppo. 'I should like to have such a purse.'

'I am sure you would,' the man told him, 'but I doubt if there is another purse like this in all the world. And I am certainly not going to give this one away.'

'I suppose not,' Beppo agreed thoughtfully. 'However, since you have the purse, I don't suppose you will mind paying the bill for both of us?'

'With pleasure,' said the other man, and he turned around to look for the landlord, leaving the magic purse lying on the table. Beppo immediately seized it and ran away out of the village as fast as he could, with the indignant owner in pursuit. Burdened as he was by his knapsack, Beppo was not as fast as the man he had just robbed. But when he saw that the other was about to overtake him he simply opened the mouth of the knapsack and said – 'Jump in!'

Once the stranger was safely inside the bag, Beppo pointed out to him that he must have been in possession of the purse for some time and had undoubtedly done very well out of it. Now it was time for someone else to enjoy its magic properties. The owner of the purse did not altogether agree with this argument. But when he discovered that he could not possibly get out of the bag unless Beppo released him there was nothing he could do except to promise that if Beppo set him free he would give up all right to the magic purse. Then Beppo let him out, wished him Godspeed, and went happily on his own way, with both the knapsack and the purse.

He stayed at home for about two years. In that time

he did a great deal of good with the magic purse, for he had a kind heart and was always ready to help anyone in distress, and a great deal of mischief with the knapsack. If anyone disagreed with him he had only to say – 'Jump in!' – in order to get his own way; people very soon realized that they would do well to give him anything he wanted, or do anything he asked them to, without arguing about it. After two years of this agreeable life, however, Beppo began to get bored and restless, and he set off again for the capital to see what new adventures he could find there.

What was his surprise on reaching the capital to discover that the streets of the city were all draped in black and all its people were in mourning. When he asked what the trouble was he was told that that very night the Devil was coming to carry away the King's daughter; she must be given up to him because of a foolish vow her father the King had made many years before, without knowing what he was doing.

Beppo went to see the King at once. 'You are my benefactor,' he said, 'and the least I can do for you is to save your daughter from the Devil.'

'That is very kind of you, I am sure,' said the King, 'but I really do not see what you or anyone else can do. A bargain is a bargain, however unfairly I was tricked into it in the first place.'

'Just leave it to me,' Beppo assured him confidently, 'and you will see. But you must let me have a room next to that of the Princess, so that the Devil cannot get at her without going past me, and you must give me a table, a stick, a pen, some ink and some paper.'

The King was not very hopeful of the outcome, but he did as Beppo asked. Beppo established himself in the room next to that of the Princess, with the window open, and his knapsack open beside the window. Just before midnight there was a terrific roar, a tempest that swept the whole city with blasts of thunder and lightning, and the Devil swept in through the open window – straight into the knapsack, for Beppo had managed to cry out 'Jump in!' at just the right moment.

'What are you doing here?' Beppo asked the Devil as soon as the latter had stopped roaring and quieted down a little.

'None of your business,' he retorted.

'Oh yes, it is,' said Beppo. 'Unless I am very much mistaken, you are here to carry away the Princess, the daughter of our King, and I am here to stop you from doing it. Now then, will you swear that if I let you out you will never molest the Princess again?'

'Certainly not,' cried the Devil. 'The Princess belongs to me, from midnight tonight. I have a written agreement to that effect, signed by her father the King.'

'I know you have,' said Beppo calmly, 'that is exactly why I am here. For the last time, if I let you out of this sack, will you promise to renounce the agreement?'

'You just stop meddling in my affairs and let me out of here,' said the Devil. 'The Princess is mine, and I am not going to give her up in any circumstances.'

'We'll see about that,' said Beppo, and he took up the stick and started beating the Devil as hard as he could. Now the Devil, in Hell, has no feelings at all and no matter what you did to him it would not hurt him. But when the Devil comes to earth on an errand such as carrying away a Princess, he has to take on human form and he can feel pain just as much as an ordinary man would do; perhaps even more, being so unused to it. He was completely helpless inside the sack and all he could do was to scream and roar and finally beg for mercy, promising that if he was released he would agree not to carry off the Princess.

'Now let me out of here at once,' he demanded angrily.

'Oh no,' said Beppo, 'not so fast. You may be able to outwit a king, but I know better than to trust the Devil's word alone.'

He opened the door of the room and summoned the King and several of his courtiers to bear witness to what the Devil said. Then he prepared the paper, and pen and ink, and he made the Devil put out his hand while he was still securely confined in the sack, and write as Beppo dictated:

'I, the very Devil, herewith promise that I will never carry away Her Royal Highness the Princess, nor will I ever molest her in any way in the future. Satan, Spirit of Hell.'

Then Beppo was satisfied. He opened the knapsack and the Devil went out of the window in a cloud of dark, sulphur-smelling smoke. The King and the Queen and the Princess and all the courtiers crowded around him and thanked him and congratulated him, and praised him, until poor Beppo was really quite embarrassed. He stayed at the palace just long enough to be the guest of honour at a banquet which the King gave to celebrate his daughter's escape. Then he went on his way again.

Not long after this Beppo decided that he was tired of wandering and that he would settle down for the rest of his life in a place of his own choosing. He travelled the length and breadth of the country, from east to west and

The Devil went out of the window in a cloud of dark, sulphur-smelling smoke.

north to south, and at last he found a cottage he liked, with a garden and an orchard and a river nearby, and woods behind it. 'This suits me,' he said to himself. 'I shall stay here for the rest of my life, with my purse and my knapsack, and I shall want for nothing.'

There was some little difficulty with the police at first, because all residents in the country were supposed to have proof of their identity and the only thing that Beppo would say when they asked him who he was and what he did for a living was – 'I am myself. Who else could I be?' Finally, however, he condescended to add, 'If you want to know anything more about me, just write to the King and tell him my name.'

The indignant police wasted no time in writing to the King about this man, whom they were sure must be an impostor of some kind. And the King wasted no time in writing back and ordering them to let Beppo do anything in the world he wanted to; never to annoy him or disturb him in any way. After that, Beppo was treated with great respect by everyone.

Many years went by. Beppo enjoyed his life, as well he might, since there was almost nothing that the magic knapsack and the magic purse between them could not provide for him. Then one day a stranger, dark, quiet, and melancholy of expression, came to see him.

'Who are you?' asked Beppo.

'I am Death.'

'Oh,' said Beppo, who was by no means ready to die yet. 'Well, in that case, jump in!' – and he opened wide the mouth of the knapsack.

Death was inside the knapsack for a year and a half. Beppo did him no harm; on the contrary he made him as comfortable as was possible under the circumstances, tried to make friends with him, and often sat down beside the sack to talk to his captive. But however much Death threatened him, argued with him, or begged him to open up the sack, Beppo would not let him out.

As a result no one anywhere on earth died during that year and a half. Men and women who had been expected to live for only a few more days or even hours lived on and on and on, no one who was in any kind of an accident ever died of his wounds, and doctors found to their surprise that no matter what they prescribed for their most hopeless patients the cure was always successful. Soldiers went on fighting battles but no one was ever killed in them.

This state of affairs could not last for ever. As Death went on pointing out to Beppo over and over again, whenever he had a chance to make himself heard, it was impossible to have a world without death. It was impossible that the old, and the ill, and the unhappy should live for ever; in any case there would never be room enough on the earth for all mankind if no one ever died.

Finally Beppo had to admit that his prisoner was right. He could see for himself that it would cause endless confusion and suffering if no one ever died at all. So he let Death out of the sack, on the understanding that he would never come anywhere near Beppo Pipetta again unless he was sent for. Death readily agreed to this bargain. Then he went off about his own business in such a hurry that he vanished from Beppo's sight like a puff of smoke on the horizon. There was a great deal of work for him to catch up with, having lost a whole year and a half. That was why during the next few months war and disease suddenly broke out in every part of the world, and people seemed to be dying like flies; this went on until the number of deaths had caught up with the number that should have taken place, and could not, while Death was a prisoner.

Beppo lived for years and years and years after that. But there came a time when he lost his taste for life. He had become an old man. All his friends and his friends' children and his friends' grandchildren were dead. His benefactor the King had died long since, and the Princess he had saved from the Devil was also dead. So he sent his servant to tell Death that he was now ready for him, and that Death could come and collect his soul any time he liked.

'Certainly not!' said Death, and he sent the servant back. 'Nothing in the world would persuade me to go anywhere near that man again.'

When he heard this, Beppo set off to find Death for himself. He travelled a long way, and took many a wrong turning in the road, for there was no one who could tell him where Death lived. No one on earth had ever gone in search of Death before except Beppo's own servant, and the servant had been so terrified that he had not been able to explain very clearly where he had been. In spite of this difficulty Beppo did finally reach the dark castle where Death lived, only to find that Death was not at home; he was busy elsewhere. He had, however, apparently left word that if a person called Beppo Pipetta ever came to see him he should be thrown out of the castle immediately, and the more roughly his servants treated Beppo the more pleased Death would be. The servants therefore pushed him out the castle door, and down the steps, warning him to go away and never come back again.

'What an ungrateful wretch this Death is,' exclaimed Beppo. 'I tried to be so nice to him. I would have done better to keep him in the sack after all.'

He sighed and went on his way, wondering what to do next. But he soon cheered up again. 'Ah well,' he thought to himself, 'if I can't die I shall have to go straight to Hell. That is undoubtedly where Death would have sent me.'

He reached Hell without any difficulty. The road there was broad, straight and well marked. But when the Devil heard who was asking for admittance he cried out – 'What! That man? Tell him to go away from here at once and never show his face again. I would rather close the gates of Hell for ever than have Beppo Pipetta inside of them.' So the servants of Satan fell upon poor Beppo, and beat him, and threw him out of Hell.

'That settles it,' said Beppo, bruised but not altogether downhearted. 'If I cannot die and I cannot get into Hell, I will have to go to Heaven.'

He tidied himself as best he could and presented himself at the gates of Paradise, where he explained his difficulties to Saint Peter.

'Well,' said Saint Peter, shaking his head and running his fingers through his beard, 'I don't know what to say. I will have to go and ask the Lord. I doubt very much whether He will agree to your being allowed to enter Heaven in such an unorthodox way.'

While Saint Peter was gone Beppo waited patiently outside. He could not go through the gate, which was guarded by angels, and he knew better than to try to climb over the wall, even though it was not very high. No one had any hope of entering Heaven without permission. But what he did do was to throw his cap over the wall, so that it landed in the gardens of Paradise.

When Saint Peter came back Beppo could see at once that he brought bad news. 'The Lord says you cannot come in here,' the Saint told him, reluctantly, for he had taken a liking to Beppo and he did not see what the poor man could do if he was not allowed into either Heaven or Hell. 'He is sorry you are in such a sad plight but, you see, we really do have to abide by the regulations and there is nothing in the regulations that covers your case. Except for the fact that you once beat the Devil, you seem to have no qualifications for Heaven.'

'Oh well, never mind,' said Beppo, with apparent resignation. 'I suppose I shall just have to go on living for ever, and make the best of it. Some people would probably be glad to live for ever.'

He turned to go away. Then he turned back as though he had suddenly remembered something. 'Before I go,' he said, 'Do you mind if I just come inside and pick up my cap? It blew over the wall there.'

'Of course not,' said Saint Peter.

So Beppo stepped through the gate, went over to where his cap was lying on the ground, and sat down upon it. 'You are quite right about the regulations,' he told the astonished Saint, 'I know something about regulations myself. And one thing I know is that if a man is on his own property, wherever it may be, no one else can order him to get off it. Now you wouldn't say that a man's hat was not his own property, would you?'

Saint Peter laughed. He went and told the Lord what had happened, and the Lord laughed too. 'Let him stay,' He said. 'If even a few inches of Paradise belong to him, he might as well enjoy the whole of it.'

TWO

The Mysterious Letter

Not so very long ago a certain rich man who owned a great deal of property some miles outside Rome, towards the east, died and left his entire estate to his son. There were vineyards, orchards and fields, there were herds of cattle and flocks of sheep, there was a castle and there were innumerable villas and pleasure houses and farmers' cottages scattered throughout the land. The son, who also became a Count upon his father's death, was pleased enough to have all this, but he took it very much for granted. He had always expected that he would eventually inherit his father's estates, and he accepted them as though they belonged to him by right. It did not even occur to him to have a Mass said in church for the repose of his father's soul.

Some time after this rich man had died a very poor man was walking home from work through the streets of Rome and he stopped, as he did each evening, to say a prayer in the church of Santa Maria Maggiore. This is one of the most beautiful churches in Rome, and one of the largest, its graceful domes and tall campanile, or bell tower, being visible from almost every part of the city. Yet it is a friendly church. The poor man never felt overwhelmed by its size; on the contrary he felt his heart uplifted by the lightness of the dome above him, the bright candles, and the feeling of warmth inside.

On this occasion, however, he was too unhappy to take any pleasure in the beauty of the candle-lit church. He had just lost his job. He was on his way home to tell his wife that he was out of work again, and that he had no idea when or where he would be able to find anything else to do. They were already so poor that it was all he could do to keep his family fed even when he did have a job; now winter was coming and it would soon be bitterly cold. So he knelt and prayed that somehow or other he would earn enough money in the next few months to support his wife and children and buy them some warm clothes.

'Nothing else,' he thought to himself; 'Just food, and warm clothes. It is not very much to ask.'

As he left the church he went on thinking to himself, half-aloud, about his misfortunes. 'I doubt if anyone else in the world is poorer than I am,' he thought, but even as he said this his eye fell upon an alms box beside the door of the church, where offerings were made for the souls of the dead in Purgatory, and he suddenly stopped.

'Indeed,' he said, still talking to himself, 'there are others worse off than I am, if they are dead and have no one to pray for their souls.' And he dropped the last farthing he had into the alms box.

He had scarcely left the church and walked down the long flight of steps to the street when a dignified and well-dressed stranger started to speak to him. Thinking that there was some mistake, since so prosperous a gentleman could not possibly have anything to say to him, the poor man paid no attention and went his own way. Then the other man stopped him, saying:

'You have done me so much good, how is it that now you do not speak to me?'

'I?' he asked in amazement, 'When have I done good to you?'

'Just now,' said the stranger.

'I am sure I do not know what you are talking about,' the poor man protested, afraid that this misunderstanding might lead him into trouble. 'How could a man like myself have been of any service to your excellency?'

'Never mind,' said the other. 'If you do not remember, that is nothing to worry about. But perhaps you would be good enough to do me one other small service?'

'Of course, of course. Anything you say.'

The stranger handed him a letter, addressed to a certain Count, at a certain palace. 'Please deliver this for me,' he said, and he told him exactly where the palace was and how to get there. 'But you must insist on giving it into the hands of the Count himself. Whoever stops you, whatever they say, you must refuse to hand it over to anyone else at all.'

'I will do as you say,' the poor man promised.

He wasted no time in setting off on the errand he had been given. He stopped by at his own home on the way – and a poor enough home it was, just one room in a tumbledown cottage that was scarcely better than a stable – long enough to tell his wife not to worry if he was away for two or three days. But he did not tell her that he had lost his job. 'Because,' he thought to himself, 'if I deliver this letter safely, and if it carries good news, the Count will surely give me some kind of a reward.

Who knows; we might even be able to live all winter on what he gives me.'

So it was with a light heart that the poor man made his way out of the east gate of the city and along the ancient road leading towards the hills. He asked the way of everyone he met along the road, and by afternoon of the following day he had reached his destination. This turned out to be a handsome palace, standing at the end of a long avenue of cypress trees and surrounded by lawns and flower gardens, with fountains splashing and little brooks trickling through specially designed rock gardens. The sun cast long shadows from the trees, late roses were still blooming in front of the palace, and altogether the poor man thought that this was one of the most attractive places he could imagine.

He did not, however, receive a very warm welcome. The porter at the gate, who was dressed in a smart uniform and held himself very stiff and straight, was obviously in the habit of turning away strangers and beggars. He haughtily demanded what the poor man wanted.

'I have a letter for the Count,' he said.

The porter looked at him in surprise, and his manner became a little less haughty.

'Very well,' he said. 'I will deliver it to him.'

'I am afraid that I must deliver it into his own hands,' said the poor man. 'I have strict instructions to that effect.'

'That is impossible,' said the porter, and he summoned the major-domo of the palace, a man dressed in livery, with a cocked hat and an air of great importance.

'I have a letter for the Count,' the poor man told him, 'which I must deliver into his own hands.'

The major-domo looked him up and down scornfully. 'Impossible,' he said. 'You cannot see the Count.'

'If I cannot see the Count, then he will never have the letter,' said the poor man. He did not want to make trouble, but he had promised to deliver the letter in person and he was determined to deliver the letter in person or not at all. He went on saying this over and over again, until finally the porter and the major-domo summoned the Count's personal valet, the most important (and the most conceited) servant in all the palace staff. They explained the situation to him and he held out his hand to the poor man:

'Give it to me, my good fellow,' he said. 'You may rest assured that it will be delivered safely. In fact,' he went on, 'I am so close to the Count that we might as well be one and the same person.'

'That may be,' said the poor man stubbornly, 'although I do not quite see how two people can be one and the same. But I have orders to give this letter into the hands of the Count, and no one else.'

The valet was so angry at this that he tried to seize the letter, the poor man resisted, the porter and the major-domo joined in the scuffle, and they all made such a noise that the Count himself came out to see what was the matter. Then of course he heard the whole story, and agreed to receive the letter.

No sooner had he seen the handwriting on the envelope than the Count turned very pale. He turned it over and over in his hands as though he did not dare open it. At last he tore it open and read it once, twice and three times.

'Who gave you this letter?' he demanded.

'I really do not know,' said the poor man. 'It was a

well-dressed gentleman who stopped me as I was coming out of Santa Maria Maggiore yesterday and asked me to be sure and give this letter personally to your Excellency.'

'I see,' said the Count. 'Would you recognize this man if you saw him again?'

'Indeed I would. His manner was so curious, and it seemed so strange that he should want to speak to me, that I looked closely into his face.'

'Come with me,' said the Count, and he turned and led the way back into the palace. The porter and the valet and the major-domo started to follow him but he waved them back and the two men went up the great staircase alone. At the head of the staircase the Count turned right and went down a long, long corridor, up another staircase, and finally into a room with very high ceilings, which was apparently a picture gallery. Both sides of the room were hung with portraits, portraits of both men and women, young and old, some in modern dress and some in the costumes of long ago. These were portraits of the Count's family, including his ancestors for many generations past.

The Count stopped just inside the door of the room. 'Does any picture here resemble the man who sent you?' he demanded. 'Look carefully, and take your time. I must know the truth.'

The poor man walked down one side of the room, and back along the other, looking closely at the portraits. No sooner had his eyes fallen on a small painting hanging on the north side of the room than he stopped in front of it. 'This is the man,' he said; 'There can be no doubt about it. Not only would I know him anywhere, but he was wearing this very same costume when I saw him yesterday.'

The Count put his hand on the back of a chair to steady himself, for he was trembling. 'That is my father,' he cried. 'My father who died six months and more ago. I did not think I could have mistaken his handwriting.'

Now it was the turn of the poor man, staring at him, to tremble. 'Do you mean that the man who handed me this letter yesterday was dead?' he exclaimed.

'He was dead. Sit down, and I will read you the letter.'

The poor man sat down gratefully, his knees feeling weak under him, but the Count continued to stand leaning against the back of the chair.

'My son,' he read, 'I commend this man to your care. Today, in the Church of Santa Maria Maggiore, he gave a farthing so that prayers could be said for the souls of the dead in Purgatory, among whom I am numbered. He is a poor man, and it was his last farthing. So it seems that it is only the poor who remember the dead, while the rich have forgotten us.

'For this reason I ask you, my son, to take this poor man and his family into your house and to support them, providing food, clothing and shelter for them as long as they live.'

When he heard this the poor man said nothing. He could not think of anything to say. 'You see,' the Count went on, 'it never occurred to me, his own son, to give anything for the peace of my father's soul. How easy it is to forget the dead, who can no longer speak to us!'

'But he did speak,' the poor man protested.

Then the Count laughed in spite of himself. 'You are right,' he said. 'Thank Heaven, this time it is not too late to make up for my thoughtlessness.'

He summoned the porter and the valet and the major-domo and ordered them to provide good lodgings for the poor man overnight. Next day he gave him a cottage of his own, not far from the palace grounds, where he could bring his wife and children, and appointed him head gardener of the whole estate. He and his children and his grandchildren lived on as gardeners there, and some of his great-grandchildren live there still.

But that was not all. The Count ordered Mass to be said that very day in the palace chapel in memory of his father. Thereafter he invariably contributed a certain part of the income from all his estates to the Church of Santa Maria Maggiore, so that prayers might be said daily for his father and for all other souls who might be in Purgatory. Nor did he himself ever again forget to pray for them.

THREE

The Frog

IN THE OLD days, and even quite recently, enchantment was much more common than it is now. People were never quite sure what they might find over the next hill or even at the bottom of their own well. Maidens and young men were often laid under a spell which turned them into an animal or a bird, or even an ogre, and sometimes birds and animals might take on human shape either for a short time or for ever. Witches were both good and bad. Magic was found in the most unlikely places, and a wise man was one who was never surprised by anything.

We must not think of enchantment as something that only happened to kings and princesses and noblemen. We may hear more about enchanted princesses than ordinary girls, but that is because whatever happened to the kings and princesses was talked about everywhere and more people heard their stories than if they had been common folk. Magic adventures might take place in a peasant's cottage just as well as in a palace.

Nor must we think that the peasants were always poor and unfortunate. Although some of them did have a very hard time making ends meet and supporting their families, others were quite well off, or at least they had everything they needed, and more besides. Once upon a time for instance there was a peasant woman who lived with her three sons in a very pleasant, large cottage in a prosperous part of the country. The soil there was fertile, rain fell regularly, and the woman and her sons made a good living. They envied no one, not even the king of the country.

The mother was a very careful and good housewife. She could spin and she could cook and she could weave fine linen. Her house was always spotlessly clean. And she was determined that when her sons got married they should all three find wives who would look after them as well as she had done.

Now the time came when the two older sons fell in love with two pretty girls. They decided to tell their mother that they wanted to get married. So they said to the younger brother, 'Come with us and we will all three ask our mother for permission to get married at the same time,' and he agreed, even though he had never yet spoken to a girl in his life, except perhaps to say 'Good morning'.

The three brothers went along together and asked their mother for permission to marry, but the two eldest did not say that they had already chosen their brides, nor did the youngest say that he had not. They just said that they all thought it was time they were looking for good wives. Their mother, taking it for granted that if they wanted to marry they each had some particular girl in mind, agreed with them.

'I have been thinking the same thing,' she said. 'It is high time you were married, and each had a wife of your own to weave your sheets, and mend your shirts, and cook your *pasta* and *polenta* for you. Only mind you choose good housewives, who will look after you well.'

As she said this she picked up three skeins of flax and gave one to each of her sons. 'Take this to whatever girl you may be thinking of marrying, and ask her to weave you a length of fine linen,' she told them. 'Then we will see how good a wife she would make you.'

The two eldest sons took the flax to their intended brides, who gladly agreed to weave it into fine linen for them. But the youngest son did not know what to do. He was too shy to confess to his mother, or even his brothers, that he did not know any girls at all and had certainly never thought of asking one to marry him. He wandered unhappily down the village street, and once or twice when he met a young girl he summoned up his courage and asked her whether she would not weave the flax for him, but each one only laughed and joked and said she had no time to go off weaving linen for a youth she had never seen before.

He went on walking and walking, until he was a long way from the village, and he came to a pond, and there he sat down on the bank of the pond and began to weep bitterly. The next thing he knew he heard a plop, as though something had fallen into the water, and a frog was sitting beside him.

'Why do you weep?' the frog asked him.

It did not occur to him to be surprised that the frog could talk. He told her what had happened; how his two brothers had taken the flax to their fiancées to be woven, and how he had no one to weave his flax for him.

'That is nothing to be unhappy about,' said the frog. 'I will weave you the finest piece of linen you ever saw.'

'Why do you weep?' the frog asked him.

Thereupon she took the skein of flax and disappeared into the pond.

Time passed. One day the mother said to her three sons, 'By now the girls you have chosen to marry must have finished weaving the flax you gave them. Go and bring me the linen they have woven, so that I can judge how good it is.'

The oldest brother and the second brother went to see their fiancées and each one came back with a piece of fine linen, white and well woven. Meanwhile the youngest son went off by himself and came to the pond, and sat down there, and sighed. He did not believe that a frog who lived in the bottom of a pond would have been able to weave linen out of flax.

'Well, what are you sighing for? Here is your linen,' said a voice beside him. There was the frog, and she had with her a piece of beautiful, fine white linen. The boy took it back to his mother, who exclaimed that this was by far the finest of the three and that the youngest son must have found a very light-fingered and clever girl to be his wife.

'But it is one thing to weave,' she said, 'and another to sew. Now take this material here' – and she gave them each a length of cloth – 'and ask the girls you love to make you each a shirt.'

The two older brothers went off again to their fiancées. And again the younger brother went to the edge of the pond, and wept. But he kept one eye open, for he hoped that if the frog could help him once, she could help him twice. Sure enough, he had not shed more than a dozen tears when the frog appeared beside him.

'Why do you weep?' she asked him again, and he told her.

'That is nothing to be unhappy about,' she said. 'You shall have a finer shirt than either of your brothers.'

So when the time came for the three brothers to bring home the three shirts the youngest brother went down to the pond again, and waited. There was a loud plop, and the frog appeared beside him carrying a beautifully made shirt. He tried it on at once. It fitted him perfectly; moreover, the stitches were so fine that they were almost invisible, and the seams were so narrow that it looked as though the material had actually been woven together there. Overjoyed, the young lad thanked the frog warmly and went dancing home to show it off to his mother.

'That is the best made shirt I have ever seen,' she exclaimed. Even his two brothers, although they both had shirts very nicely tailored and sewn, could not help admitting that the youngest brother's shirt was the best.

'However, there is still one thing more,' said their mother. 'I must know whether these three girls you have chosen are capable of bringing up their children well. Now here are three small puppies. Each of you take one of these to your intended bride and ask her to train it and bring it up as best she can. When the dogs are full grown we will judge how well their mistresses have trained them.'

The three brothers each set off with a puppy in their arms. But the younger brother had no idea what to do next. It was one thing to weave and sew; it was quite another to expect even the most remarkable frog to bring up a lively animal several times larger than herself. Nevertheless he wandered down to the pond again, and sat on the bank, and wept, while the puppy frisked and played about beside him.

The next thing he knew he heard the familiar plop and the frog was there again. 'Why are you weeping?' she asked, and he told her.

'That is nothing to be unhappy about,' said the frog; 'I will bring up the puppy for you.' Before he could say anything else she whispered something in the little dog's ear, and she and the puppy both disappeared into the pond before his very eyes.

Time passed. At length, after many months had gone by, the mother said to her three sons: 'Those three dogs must be full grown by now. Go and fetch them and bring them here, and I will see how well trained they are.'

The oldest brother and the second brother went to see their fiancées, and each came back with a handsome, full-grown dog. The two dogs were well enough trained, and obedient, and well-groomed, but they were both inclined to be rough and unfriendly with strangers and had to be kept on the lead most of the time. Meanwhile the younger son had gone back to the pond again, thinking that his own puppy must have been drowned long since, yet hoping against hope that by some miracle the frog had been able to keep it alive until it was fully grown.

This time the frog was already waiting for him. With her was the handsomest dog he had ever seen. It was not only handsome. It was so lively and intelligent that it really seemed to understand everything you said to it, and would roll over, or bark, or sit up and beg for food, or do anything else you could think of; moreover, it seemed gentle and friendly towards everyone.

The youth promptly took his dog back to his mother, who was delighted. 'All the dogs have learned to obey, which is the most important thing,' she said. 'But the others, as so often happens, have lost their youthful friendliness and playfulness, while this little dog is still sweet and playful and natural as well as obedient. It is the most beautiful dog I have ever seen.'

The youngest son was of course very happy to hear this. But his happiness did not last long. His mother went on to say that now she was satisfied that all her three future daughters-in-law would make good wives and housewives, there was no reason to delay the weddings any longer. The three brothers should go and fetch their brides home as soon as possible, while she prepared the wedding feast. As you can imagine, the youngest son simply did not know what to say. Now he would certainly be found out. He wandered miserably down to the pond again, not because he had much hope that the frog could help him this time, but because he did not know where else to go. How, he thought to himself in despair, how could he tell his mother and his brothers that it was a frog who had woven his flax into linen, sewn his shirt so skilfully, and brought up the dog for him? They would never stop laughing.

He sat down on the bank and wept more bitterly than he had ever wept before. Immediately the frog appeared at his side. 'Why are you weeping so sadly?' she asked him, and he told her.

'That is nothing to be unhappy about,' she said. 'I will marry you.'

When he heard this the youth was even more miserable than before. He was grateful to the frog for all she had done to help him, but he really did not see how he could take a frog to be his wife. 'How can I possibly marry you?' he said.

'Do not ask me that,' she said. 'Just answer me: will you marry me, or will you not?'

'How could I refuse you anything, after all the wonderful things you have done for me?' he replied, trying not to look as unhappy as he felt. 'If you wish me to marry you, then marry you I will.'

At that the frog disappeared. Now if this were an ordinary fairy story, she would probably have been transformed into a beautiful maiden there and then, as soon as he spoke the words. But such transformations are not always easy to bring about. When she returned a moment later, the frog was still a frog. She had, however, brought with her a very handsome small carriage, drawn by two tiny white horses.

'Come with me,' she said, hopping into the carriage. He had some difficulty following her, because the carriage was so very small, being more suitable for a frog than a man to travel in, but he managed to step inside and he sat down beside her as best he could. They drove away in the direction of the village.

Before they had gone very far along the road they met three witches. One of the witches was blind, for her eyelids had grown together until she could no longer open them. The second witch was a hunchback. And the third witch had such a large thorn stuck in her throat that she could not open her mouth and could scarcely even breathe.

When the three witches saw the little carriage driving towards them, and they saw that inside the carriage, sitting up very straight on silk cushions, was a frog, they started to laugh. At least the second and third witches, who could see, started to laugh and then they told the first witch, who was blind, what they were laughing at and she laughed just as hard as the others. They laughed and laughed and laughed. Finally they fell into such fits of laughter that the eyes of the first witch flew open and she recovered her sight; the second witch rolled over and over and over on the ground, laughing, until she found her back unexpectedly straightened out; and the third witch laughed so hard that she choked and the thorn was dislodged from her throat.

By the time the witches had stopped laughing the carriage was so far ahead of them on the road that it was almost out of sight. But as soon as they realized what had happened they flew after it, determined to reward the frog who had thus unintentionally made them all three well again. (Or perhaps it was not unintentional; there was no doubt that the frog had a great deal of magic of her own.)

The first witch waved her wand over the frog, who immediately changed into the most beautiful girl you could imagine, with honey-coloured hair flowing down over her shoulders, and eyes bluer than the sea; she was wearing a green and gold dress, with golden slippers on her feet. The second witch waved her wand over the carriage and the horses, which immediately doubled in size and became a magnificent open carriage, drawn by four large white horses. The third witch waved her wand and a magic purse, filled with money, appeared out of the air.

'For your dowry,' she said, putting it into the hands of the transformed frog.

Without even waiting for the girl to say thank you, the witches vanished. So the youngest son found himself with a beautiful bride, a carriage, four horses, and all the money they both could use. They wasted no time in driving home to his mother's house, where his two older brothers had already brought their brides, and the three sons were married in turn on that day, and the next day, and the day after that, with three wedding feasts.

The mother was delighted with her three daughters-in-law, all of whom were industrious, clever and lovely to look at. But there was no doubt which one she liked the best. For the rest of her life she kept telling her youngest son how lucky he was, and how clever she herself had been.

'I was wise to set you and your brothers those tests,' she would say, 'for they proved beyond any doubt that you had all chosen wives who were worthy of you. And they certainly made it clear to me that the girl you loved was the most remarkable of the three. As soon as I saw the linen, the shirt, and the dog, I knew that you had found the most wonderful girl in the world.'

The youngest son, wisely, never told his mother just how he had found the most wonderful girl in the world.

FOUR

The Thoughtless Abbot

FORTUNE, OR LUCK, often seems to choose favourites. One man may work all his life and yet remain poor, while his neighbour, who is not necessarily either more virtuous, more industrious or wiser than the first man, will become richer and richer.

So it was in one of the smaller Italian cities not long ago. Among the priests living in that city there was one who always managed to have the best of everything. Even as a young man he seemed to have a golden touch. Whatever he did, prospered, and whatever he wished for seemed to come true. In due course he became the Abbot of a wealthy monastery outside the city, which in those days meant that he had control of great estates and command of a great many people, not only priests but also secretaries, clerks, farmers, servants and shepherds.

As Abbot, he was one of the most important men in the entire kingdom. There was nothing in the world that he did not have. He lived like a prince, in beautifully furnished apartments, with servants to do everything for him; stewards and valets and gardeners and cooks and stable-boys and coachmen. Even his robes, although they were cut in the simple style suitable to an Abbot, were of the finest material to be found in Italy.

It must be admitted that the Abbot enjoyed himself. Although he was a priest, he did not believe in austerity for the sake of austerity, and he was ready to make the most of whatever good fortune came his way. He liked good food and drink, he liked to sit around talking to his friends until late at night, and he did not like to do any work at all. On the other hand he was always very kind to his servants, from the lowest to the highest, and treated them all well, so that everyone in the monastery liked him. They laughed at his idle ways, and they nicknamed him 'The Thoughtless Abbot' because he paid so little attention to anything except his own pleasures, but they did not resent the fact that he was so rich and so lazy and so happy in his idleness.

Outside the monastery it was different. There were a great many other priests, and laymen too, who were jealous of the Abbot. Why should he live in such luxury, they asked one another, while they had worked hard all their lives and had nothing to show for it? They swore that they would get even with him, and that if ever they had a chance to do him any harm they would make the most of it.

Then one day the King passed through their city, where he stopped at an inn to refresh himself. No one knew he was coming, not even the Abbot, and no one had arranged any special entertainment for him. He simply ordered a glass of wine, and some fresh-baked bread, and sat talking to the innkeeper long enough for the coachmen to water and feed his horses, and let them rest.

This was the chance the Abbot's enemies had been

waiting for. As soon as they heard that the King had stopped at their inn several of them went to pay their respects. While they were there they said to him:

'Oh King, you should know that in this city there lives a man who is as rich as you, and perhaps richer. He is as happy as you, and perhaps happier. He has as many servants as you have, and perhaps more. Is it right that any man should enjoy prosperity as great as his King's?'

'Who is this man?' asked the King.

'He is the man we call the Thoughtless Abbot. Thoughtless, because he is so busy eating and drinking, and ordering his servants around, that he thinks of nothing else. As you see, he did not even think of coming to greet Your Majesty.'

No one mentioned that the monastery was some little distance outside the town, and that the Abbot could not possibly have heard of the King's arrival.

'I see,' said the King. He was an easy-going ruler, almost as fond of the good things of life as the Abbot himself, but no king likes to think that his subjects are lacking in respect for him. It did seem to him when he heard this story that the Abbot had been deliberately discourteous. 'Well, gentlemen, rest assured that I will give your Thoughtless Abbot something to think about.'

Then he sent for the Abbot. The Abbot came at once, wearing his finest clothes and riding in his best carriage, with the prancing, piebald horses. The King received him kindly, bade him sit down, and talked with him of this and that and many other things. The Abbot was an intelligent man, although so lazy, and the King listened with interest to what he had to say about different parts of the world and about life in his own monastery. They had a glass of wine together. But at length the King said:

'Why do they call you the Thoughtless Abbot?'

'Why, I suppose it is because I have not a single care in the world,' the Abbot replied. 'I have all the servants I need to attend to my affairs, all the money I need to support myself and my servants, all the possessions I require for my own happiness. What should I think about?'

'You might think about the next world,' suggested the King, 'or perhaps about saving your own soul.'

'Oh that I do. From Matins to Compline, from dawn to midnight, I never miss a single service at the monastery the whole day through. I pray morning and night. But those are prayers; they do not need any great thought on my part.'

'In that case, my dear Abbot, since you have so much time on your hands and so little to think about, I am sure you would be glad to do something for me?'

'With pleasure, Your Majesty. You have only to command me.'

'It is really a very small thing. I should like you to count the stars in the sky and let me know how many there are. I will give you three days and three nights in which to count them. And of course,' the King went on speaking quietly enough, but at his words the Abbot felt himself begin to quiver like the leaves of a poplar tree, 'of course, since you already have everything in the world you want there is no reward I can offer you for this service. I can only promise you that if you are not able to tell me the exact number of stars in the sky within three days I will have you beheaded then and there.'

Having said this, the King went on his way. The poor Abbot rode back to his monastery, staring up at the sky, although it was still early in the afternoon and there were no stars to be seen. He was no astronomer, but he knew perfectly well that there must be thousands and thousands of stars in the heavens. He had often sat out on his terrace on warm nights, watching the few constellations that he could recognize moving slowly across the skies. He knew the Great Bear and the Little Bear, those constellations that circle close around the North Pole and are visible almost every night in the year. He knew the Scorpion, a star-studded creature so huge and terrible that it was believed to have frightened even the horses of the Sun into stampeding when the young charioteer Phaethon tried to drive them across the sky. He knew Orion, the Giant, who in spite of his great size was also afraid of the Scorpion and would never rise above the eastern horizon until the Scorpion had set in the west, so that he only appeared in the sky in winter. And that was just about all he did know.

As soon as the sun had set and the sky began to turn deep blue he went out on his terrace and started to count the stars. At first only a few of the brighter ones were visible, and he counted those, but as the sky grew darker and still darker more and more stars kept appearing and he had to start all over again. The stars also kept moving slowly but steadily westward, in the same path as the sun and moon, so that the ones he had already counted kept disappearing and new ones rose above the horizon.

By the middle of the night the Milky Way had also risen into such a position that it stretched across the whole sky above him, and in the Milky Way alone there were hundreds and hundreds of thousands of stars. He counted and counted and counted all night.

Next morning he was so exhausted and so frightened by the threat of death hanging over his head that he could not even eat breakfast. For three days he neither ate nor drank nor spoke to anyone. Each night he went

He counted and counted all night.

out on the terrace as soon as it was dark and counted and counted and counted, knowing even as he counted that the task was impossible and that even if he counted for three years or three centuries he would never get it right.

The Abbot's servants, seing their master's strange behaviour, became more and more worried about him. 'Surely he must have lost his mind,' they said to one another, and they were almost afraid to speak to him or go near his room.

Finally on the third day a trusty old servant, who had been with the Abbot ever since he was a young man, took his courage in his hands and went to his master and begged him to confess what was troubling him. Then the Abbot broke down and told him the whole story, and how he must number the stars, and could not.

'This afternoon I must go to the King,' he said, 'and tell him that I have failed. The penalty is death.'

When he heard this the servant was almost as dismayed as his master. But not for long. 'Give me an hour, and a purse full of money,' he said, 'and I will bring you the answer.'

'Impossible,' said the Abbot. 'You cannot count the stars in broad daylight, and you certainly cannot buy the correct answer. No one on earth has ever counted the stars.'

'That is just the point,' said the servant. 'Wait for me.'

An hour later he came back, carrying with him a large brown and white ox-hide. He spread this out on the floor and while the Abbot watched in complete astonishment he cut off part of the tail, half of one ear, and a small piece from one side of the skin.

'Now,' he said. 'Take this to the King. Spread it out on the floor as I have done, and when he asks you the number of stars tell him that there are exactly as many stars as there are hairs on the ox-hide, neither more nor less. You must explain that when the hide was whole there were slightly more hairs than there were stars, which is why you have cut off part of the skin to make the number of hairs correspond exactly to that of the stars.'

The Abbott embraced him warmly. 'I think you may have saved my life,' he said, smiling for the first time in three days. Then he set off for the King's palace in his finest carriage, with two outriders, two grooms, and the precious ox-hide lying at his feet.

The King received him in the throne room, surrounded by his courtiers. A number of the Abbot's enemies had also managed to be there, for the story of the King's command had become widely known in the last three days and they hoped to witness the downfall of the man whom they had so long envied. The King first asked his visitor to sit down. Then he wasted no time in coming to the point.

'Now tell me,' he said, 'how many stars are there in the sky?' And everyone in the throne room fell silent, waiting for the answer, knowing that in fact there could be no answer.

'Your Majesty, the sum is so great that I could not carry it in my head, nor write it on any parchment. Just let me show you —' He clapped his hands and his servants came into the room, carrying the ox-hide, which they spread out on the floor. 'The number of stars in the sky, Your Majesty,' the Abbot continued, 'is exactly the number of hairs in this ox-hide.'

While the King and the entire company stared at him open-mouthed the Abbot, who was now beginning to enjoy himself, pointed out the gaps where his servants had cut off pieces of the skin. 'There were originally more hairs here than there are stars in the heavens, so I have cut off the extra ones. The number is now identical. Of course if you are not satisfied with this,' he went on, with a slight twinkle in his eye, 'you can ask someone else to count the stars as well, and we will compare notes.'

The King was delighted. He had taken a liking to the easy-going Thoughtless Abbot, and he was beginning to suspect that the men who had originally spoken against him had spoken out of jealousy. He certainly

His servants came into the room, carrying the ox-hide.

had no wish to have to carry out his threat and order the Abbot beheaded.

'Go your way in peace,' he told him, 'and live as long as Noah or Methusaleh, without thoughts, for if this is what comes of not thinking we would all do well to think less.'

The Abbot and the King remained good friends for

the rest of their lives, enjoying each other's company. The envious little group of men who had plotted against the Abbot went on being envious, and complaining, and feeling sorry for themselves, but there was nothing they could do about it as long as he enjoyed the King's favours. The Thoughtless Abbot remained happy and carefree as long as he lived.

Yet he was not altogether thoughtless. He promoted the servant who had brought him the ox-hide to be his chief steward, and awarded him a special allowance of an extra ounce of silver every day, and two on Sundays. He studied astronomy and learned a great deal more about the stars than he had ever known before, although he never again tried to count them. Perhaps, also, he put a litle more thought into his daily prayers than he had been in the habit of doing before.

FIVE

The Dark King

SOUTHERN ITALY is a poor country. It is stony and dry. Its rocky hillsides will support olive groves, and lemon and orange groves, but there is little of the rich farmland that is to be found in the north. Its people are, for the most part, poor and hard-working. The poorest and hardest working of all – at least until quite recently – were those who earned their living by gathering chicory.

Chicory is a plant which is not only cultivated but also grows wild in some parts of Italy. Its leaves resemble those of lettuce and are often used in salads. But it is not an easy plant to find. The chicory-gatherer must wander far afield, working in all weathers, and even when he has collected as much chicory as he can carry it does not fetch a very high price in the market.

At the time our story begins, a hundred years ago and more, there was one chicory-gatherer who was even poorer than most. Although his wife and his three daughters all worked with him, and they had a little donkey to help them carry the chicory to market, they could barely earn enough money to feed themselves and the donkey. One day, just before the beginning of the three-day Carnival which takes place every year in spring (and is followed by Lent, when everyone fasts for forty days) this man said to his family:

'We must start work early tomorrow, and work late. At Carnival time the price of chicory is high; we might be able to make a little extra money.'

Next morning, therefore, he and his wife and his daughters went off early, and in different directions, trying to cover as much ground as quickly as they could.

Now it happened that the youngest daughter went farther than any of the others. She was a long way from home, and a long way from either her sisters or her parents, when she came upon the largest, finest chicory plant she had ever seen. She pulled it up very carefully, roots and all. What was her astonishment to find that as she did so it left a great hole in the earth, like the entrance to a cave. At first she thought perhaps it was in fact a cave. But when she looked down into the hole she could see beneath her what looked like the dining-room of a great palace. The room was lit by silver candelabra, and there was a long table in the centre, covered with fine linen and set with china, glass and silver. To her surprise she saw that it was set for only one person. And then she suddenly noticed, what she had not seen before, that there was a golden staircase leading down from where she stood into the room below.

She was cold and hungry. She looked around her, but there was no one else anywhere in sight. So she took her courage in her hands, climbed quietly down the steps, and found herself alone in what was indeed an elegant dining-room. No sooner had she stepped into the room than an excellent, three-course dinner appeared on the table before her, apparently from nowhere. She sat down and ate, until she could eat no more, and as soon as she had finished the table was cleared away by magic; she neither saw nor heard anyone.

Less frightened now, she set out to explore the rest of the palace. She wandered through room after room after room, each one more richly furnished than the last. There was everything that anyone could wish for, not only furniture and lamps and mirrors and carpets, but also warm blankets and soft pillows, clothes and furs and jewels.

'How wonderful it would be to have some of these things in our poor hovel!' she thought to herself. 'And why not?' She quickly gathered together as much as she could carry and ran back to the dining-room, where the staircase had been. But now there was no staircase. The roof of the dining-room was as solid as that of all the other rooms in the palace. There she was alone, underground, with no apparent way of ever getting back to the earth again.

She dropped all the treasures she was carrying, and wept bitterly. Before very long, however, another delicious meal appeared on the table beside her, and she enjoyed that, and after the meal had been cleared away one of the candelabra was lifted from the table by invisible hands and led the way into a beautifully furnished bedroom nearby. There she found a warm bath waiting for her, and a deep, soft bed with sheets all made of silk. The whole room, moreover, was lined with cupboards full of the most beautiful clothes she had ever seen, or imagined, all of which fitted her perfectly.

After a good night's sleep the young chicory-gatherer decided that she might as well stop worrying and make the most of her good fortune. This new life into which she had so unexpectedly fallen was certainly pleasant.

She had nothing to do but eat and drink, dress herself in fine clothes, and admire the beauties of her underground palace.

So it went on for three months. She had every comfort and every luxury in the world; on the other hand she never saw a living soul, nor could speak to anyone. By the end of the three months she was so lonely, and sick for home, that she started to weep and simply could not stop weeping. Then the door of her room opened, slowly, and a very tall, very dark man appeared before her. He was as dark as any Moor. In fact, although she could not see his features clearly in the candlelight, she assumed that he was a Moor and her heart beat fast with fear.

The Moorish invasion of southern Italy, although it had taken place many years before this, was still remembered there. The dark-skinned, barbarian Moors who had once landed from Africa and raided the ports of southern Italy had become a legend. Mothers frightened their children with threats that they would return, and the very sight of a black man was enough to send shivers down the spine of children and adults alike.

So it was now with the young chicory-gatherer. She stared at this dark stranger, and could not speak for terror.

'Do not be afraid,' he said kindly; 'Do not weep. Why are you so unhappy here, where you have everything in the world to please you?'

'I am lonely,' she said through her tears. 'There is nothing for me to do here, all alone.'

He took out a great bunch of keys. 'You have not seen even one-tenth of the beauties of my kingdom,' he said. 'Take these, and wander wherever you like. You will find so much to entertain you here that you will never be bored again. It is all yours. There is only one room you must not enter, and that is the room without a key; if ever you open the door to that room it will go ill with you.'

Saying this, the Dark King disappeared. The girl took the keys and set forth to explore the rest of the palace, unlocking one room after another. And indeed she found so much to surprise and amuse her that for the time being she quite forgot her loneliness. She found musical instruments that played by themselves, she found games, mechanical toys, magic lanterns, and every kind of entertainment she could wish for. She found gardens, lakes, trees, in which there were birds singing; swans and geese, deer, rabbits and many other animals, all so tame that she could play with them. As she wandered here and there she often passed by the door to which there was no key, but she never tried to open it; she was an obedient young girl, and believed in doing as she was told.

Another three months went by. Then once again she was so lonely, and homesick, that she sat down in the midst of all her luxuries and pleasures and wept bitterly. Immediately the Dark King appeared beside her.

'Why are you unhappy?' he asked her.

'I am longing to see my family,' she said; 'To talk to my mother, and my father, and my sisters. I beg you, let me go home.'

'Have you forgotten how poor your home is? No comforts, no pleasures, and scarcely enough to eat.'

'I know,' she said. 'I am happy here, with the wonderful things you have given me. If only I could go home for a day, one single day, I would gladly come back to you again.'

'Very well,' he said, 'Go home for a day if that will make you happy. But promise me that you will return before the sun has set. Promise me, also, that you will not tell your sisters where you are living, nor anything about me.'

She promised. The Dark King waved his hand, and suddenly the golden staircase leading up to the surface of the earth reappeared. At the mouth of the hole above them she could see a carriage waiting, with four black horses. 'Take this to your mother,' said the King, handing her a bag filled with pieces of gold, 'and be back in good time.'

She took the gold, climbed the stairs, and stepped into the carriage. There was no coachman, but the horses set off at once in the right direction and in a very short time drew up outside the chicory-gatherer's little shack. You can imagine the amazement with which he and his wife and the two older sisters beheld such a magnificent carriage arriving at their doorstep. At first they did not recognize the younger sister; when they did they could not believe their eyes. They crowded around her, talking and laughing and asking questions. She gave her mother the bag of gold, and the poor woman wept for joy, thinking how much good food and how many new clothes she could now buy for the whole family.

In spite of all the questions they asked her the younger sister was careful not to say where she lived, or how she had got there, nor to mention the Dark King. And as soon as the sun reached the top of the tallest tree on the western horizon she said good-bye, promising to return another day, stepped into her carriage, and was back in the underground palace well before sunset.

Another three months passed. Again the girl was lonely, and again she wept. Again the Dark King appeared; again he agreed to let her go home for a single day, gave her a second bag of gold for her family, and waved his hand for the golden staircase and the carriage to appear.

This time the chicory-gatherer and his wife and daughters were not so very surprised, but they were equally delighted by the bag of gold. When they exclaimed over it, wondering how anyone could be so rich that they had gold to give away, the young girl could not help laughing.

'Why, this is nothing,' she said. 'The walls where I live are covered with gold. There are precious stones around every window. The floors are covered with carpets so thick you can scarcely walk on them; the lamps sparkle with a hundred hundred thousand diamonds.'

Her sisters, who were already jealous of her good fortune, begged her to tell them more about this wonderful palace of hers. Almost before she knew what she was saying she had told them everything – about the Dark King, about the bunch of keys she had which would open all the doors in the palace except one, and how she was forbidden to open that one. When they heard all this, her sisters were determined to see these wonders for themselves. They insisted that they would ride back in the carriage with her when she went home.

'No, no!' she cried. 'It is impossible. If the Dark King knew I had told you even this much, he would kill me. I promised never to mention it.'

'Why should it be such a secret?' the oldest sister demanded. 'What is he hiding?'

'Why of course, he must be a Moor!' cried the second sister.

'A Moor!' they repeated together, staring at their sister. 'You poor child. No wonder he hides himself away,' the elder sister went on; 'Sooner or later you may be sure he will eat you alive.'

'Unless you kill him first,' suggested the second sister. 'If only you could do that! Then we could all three live in your wonderful palace, and our parents too.'

The younger sister was horrified at this idea. At first she simply refused to listen to them. But her two sisters kept on telling her how stupid she was, and what a coward ; finally they gave her a stiletto, which is a very thin, sharp dagger, and warned her that if she did not kill the Moor with it he would certainly kill her in his own good time. She retorted that they did not know what they were talking about. Nevertheless, when she stepped into her magic coach again she took the stiletto with her.

The more she thought about what her sisters had said (and she had plenty of time to think, alone, in the empty palace), the more she was afraid they must be right. The Dark King undoubtedly was a Moor, she thought. Perhaps her life really was in danger. At last she decided that she would at least open the forbidden door, the door without a key, and see what lay behind it; whatever secret was hiden in the dark palace must be hidden there.

The door opened easily enough. It was not even locked. It opened into a room where several beautiful girls were sitting at a table, weaving the most exquisite golden cloth she had ever seen in her life. She was so surprised that she exclaimed:

'What lovely material! Who are you making it for?'

'For the bride of the Dark King,' they told her.

She went on beyond them and came to another room, where goldsmiths and silversmiths were working on the most beautiful gold and silver jewellery she had ever seen in her life.

'How lovely!' she cried. 'Who are these things for?'

'For the bride of the Dark King,' they told her.

She went on into a third room, which was dark and gloomy. There sat an old hunchback, with a pile of what looked like rags beside him, and he was patching a torn, dirty coat. 'What are you doing with that?' she asked him. 'Who would wear such old rags?'

'These are for the girl who was to have been the bride of the Dark King, when she goes away,' he told her. But she did not understand him.

Beyond the hunchback's room was a long, dark corridor; at the end of the corridor was yet another door. When she opened this last door, the girl saw the Dark King himself lying sound asleep on a couch there. And she thought to herself that now at last she could find out whether he really was as ugly and as dark and as frightening as she believed. She had never yet been able to see his face clearly.

The only light in the room was from a wax taper, stuck in a bracket on the wall. She took this down and tiptoed to the couch, with the taper in one hand and her stiletto in the other. She bent over and saw the King's face and it was as dark and as ugly as you could well imagine. Then she felt sure that her sisters were right; her Dark King was a Moor, and she must kill him.

She bent over and saw the King's face.

She raised the stiletto. As she did so the taper she was holding in her other hand wavered and a drop of wax fell on the King's face, waking him. He looked at her, he looked at the stiletto, and he sighed deeply.

'If only you had been patient a little longer,' he said, 'If only you had not opened the forbidden door, all might have been well. But it is too late now. Now you must go back to the earth, back to your hovel, back to the life of a chicory-gatherer.'

He clapped his hands. Immediately the clothes she had on vanished and she was standing there in the old dress she had been wearing when she first pulled up the great clump of chicory and found her way into the underground. A long flight of stairs, no longer golden, had appeared beside her. She turned to go, without speaking, but the King called her back.

'Nevertheless,' he said, 'take these three hairs with you. If ever you are in danger of your life burn first one, then another, then the third, and I will come to your rescue.'

Taking the three hairs, she climbed the dark stairs up to the surface of the earth. It was night there. Looking out into the darkness, she was suddenly afraid to be out alone in the fields so late, so far from home. At that moment she remembered the hunchback, and the coat he had been mending, and she begged aloud for some old, men's clothing which would serve her as a disguise. Immediately she found herself dressed from head to foot as a man, although in ragged, tattered old clothes.

Thus disguised, she made her way home. She reached there early in the morning and, waking up her parents, she tried to tell them what had happened. No one would listen to her.

'You scarecrow!' exclaimed her mother. 'How dare you pretend to be my daughter? When my daughter comes to visit us she comes in a coach of gold, with four black horses.'

Her father was even more indignant. 'Had you come begging, as an honest man, I would gladly have given you a crust of bread,' he said, 'but I will have nothing to do with a scoundrel who claims to be my daughter.' And they drove the poor girl away.

She wandered far and wide after that. At length she came to the gates of a palace and, looking inside, she saw the grooms busy rubbing down their horses in the courtyard there. So she went in. She found the head groom and asked him whether she could not learn to be a stable boy, and groom horses; and he took pity on her and let her stay. She worked there for many weeks and months, earning enough money to buy a new coat and a new suit of clothes and new shoes. But she remained always disguised as a man.

One day the Queen looked down from the palace window and noticed the new groom. She saw at once that there was something different about him, that he did not look like the other grooms, and she was much attracted by him. So she sent for him and appointed him Master of the Palace, which meant that he was in charge of all the other servants there.

Now at this time the King of the country was away at the wars, and the Queen was lonely and discontented. Before very long she fancied to herself that she was in love with this supposed man whom she had made her Master of the Palace, and she asked him to marry her if the King did not soon return from the wars.

The poor girl did not know what to say. She was afraid to tell the truth, as she should have done. She just kept saying that she was sure the King would come back soon, making one excuse after another, until finally it was quite clear that she would not agree to marry the Queen under any circumstances whatever. The Queen, thinking herself insulted, was so furious that she swore to be revenged.

So it was that when the King did at last return safely from the wars the Queen told him that while he had been away her new Master of the Palace had asked her to marry him, even threatening her with death if she refused; the King, she said, had returned home just in time to save her from such a marriage. The King believed everything she said. He therefore condemned the disguised girl to be put to death on the scaffold the very next morning.

When she heard this, the girl at last tried to explain what had happened, and why she was there disguised as a man. But no one believed her. The other servants only laughed at her and said it was a fine story she had made up, but it was certainly not going to save her life now.

Next morning she was led out to the scaffold, in front of the entire court, where the executioner was waiting for her. At the very last moment she remembered the three hairs that the Dark King had given her. She took the first one and burnt it in the flame of a torch, and suddenly there was the sound of drums in the distance and the tramp of a thousand soldiers marching. She took the second hair and burnt it, and suddenly the courtyard was filled with an army of soldiers, standing on guard around the scaffold. Then she burnt the third hair, and the Dark King himself appeared, in armour, with the visor of his helmet down so that no one could see his face.

'Why have you condemned my wife to death?' he demanded of the King.

'Your wife?' repeated the astonished King. 'Who is your wife? I know nothing about her.'

The Dark King took the pretended Master of the Palace by the hand and helped her to climb down from the scaffold. Then she told her story, telling how the Queen had attempted to force her into marriage and how she had refused. When the King heard this he knew that it was his wife who had betrayed him, and lied to him, and he ordered the faithless Queen to be executed immediately on the waiting scaffold.

Meanwhile the Dark King continued to hold the girl's hand. 'I came at your bidding, to save your life,' he said, lifting the visor of his helmet. 'But it is not true that you are my wife. You must choose now whether or not you will marry me.'

She looked at him, seeing how ugly he was, and her heart sank. Yet how could she refuse to marry him when he had just saved her life? 'Yes,' she said, 'I will marry you.'

She had scarcely spoken when she felt the earth tremble under her, as though there had been an earthquake. The next thing she knew she was standing on the steps of a Cathedral, wearing the golden wedding dress that she had seen the maidens weaving in the underground palace, with the crown and the necklace and the golden ornaments she had seen the goldsmiths making. Beside her was the Dark King. But he was no longer dark. The enchantment which had been laid upon him long, long before was to be broken as soon as a beautiful girl would, of her own free will, agree to marry him. Now that this had come to pass he was transformed again to his rightful shape, which was that of a fair and handsome youth.

Nor was this all. When they drove back after the wedding to the Dark King's underground palace, they found it no longer underground. There it stood, as beautiful and as richly furnished as before, with its golden walls and its jewelled windows, and its gardens, but it was all above ground, standing bright in the sunshine.

SIX

Nicola Pesce

THE MAINLAND OF Italy, as everyone knows, is shaped like a boot, a long, high-heeled boot sticking far out into the Mediterranean Sea. Just off the toe of the boot, in such a position that it looks like a football about to be kicked across the sea towards Gibraltar by the Italian boot is a triangular-shaped island called Sicily. Sicily is also a part of Italy, but it has a character very much its own. It is a poor country, and mountainous, and its people – whether they are shepherds or fishermen or sailors – are strong, hardy and capable of great endurance.

Because Sicily is an island, many Sicilians depend on the sea for their livelihood. They earn their living from the sea one way or another, either by fishing, or building boats, or mending nets, or sailing their ships across to the mainland and to other countries that lie far beyond. Wherever they look, their horizon is the sea.

Long, long ago, during the thirteenth century in fact, an old fisherman lived near Messina, on the northeastern tip of Sicily, just where the island is closest to the mainland. He had a great many sons, and all but one of these sons followed in their father's footsteps and became fishermen as well. The youngest son, a tall, dark-haired child, loved the sea as much as any of his brothers, or his father, but he hated to go fishing with them because he was so tender-hearted that he could not bear to see the fish dying or dead. Whenever he could he would stay at home instead, helping his mother in the garden, drawing water, chopping wood, feeding the chickens, and doing other household chores. When his work was finished he would sit down by the water's edge and watch the sea.

Occasionally his father or one of his brothers would ask him to carry the fish they had caught up to the house, or even to market, and the youngest brother – whose name was Nicola – would shoulder the heavy baskets, filled with shimmering silver fish, which they brought ashore from their fishing boats. He was very strong. The only trouble was that if ever he saw a fish moving, or giving any sign of life at all, among the shining mass of fish he would throw it back into the water in the hope that it would recover. As a result he usually arrived at the house or the market with far fewer fish than he had been given. His mother scolded him, his father scolded him, and his older brothers swore that he was the stupidest creature alive, but Nicola did not seem to mind. He would listen to what they said and then he would wander away to the seashore by himself, watching the waves and the drifting seaweed, and the seabirds skimming back and forth and flying so low that their wing-tips touched the edge of the water. He would look across to the mainland, scarcely a giant's step away from Sicily.

As he grew up Nicola spent more and more of his time at the seashore. He learned to swim, and to dive, staying under water for longer and longer periods at a time. He would come home at night and tell his brothers, and his parents, wonderful stories of what he had seen far down in the depths of the ocean. There were sunken ships, he said, with fish swimming in and out of their open portholes and seaweed growing on their decks, as though it were a garden. There were great trees of coral, both white and red, with limpets and shell-fish clinging to their rough surface; there were sea-urchins, and star-fish, and polyps and many other strange underwater creatures. And the fish! No one, said Nicola, who had not dived far under the surface of the waves had any idea what the fish were like at the bottom of the ocean. Golden fish with wide black stripes, green and purple and black fish, fish that were transparent, bright orange fish that were completely round, fish with tails that were shaped like the wings of butterflies.

Nicola's brothers listened to these tales and shrugged their shoulders, thinking that their young brother had gone mad. Even if there were strange fish to be seen under the water, they said to each other, who would want to spend his time down there in the depths? His mother and his father also came to the conclusion that perhaps Nicola was mad, and his mother was so worried about it that at length she sought out a holy man who lived in the mountains of Sicily to ask his advice.

When the holy man had heard her story, he shook his head. 'Who knows,' he said. 'It may be that your son is mad. Or it may be that this is the work of the Devil.'

'What must I do?' asked the poor woman.

'First of all you must wash his shirt in holy water,' he told her. 'And you must sew a red ribbon round his belt. You must put an acorn in his pocket. And you must give him bread to eat that has been made from darnel grass. If it is the Devil who is tormenting him, he is sure to be driven away by these things.'

The woman went home and did exactly as she had been told. She gathered darnel, which is a grass often to be found growing like a weed in cornfields, and made bread for Nicola. She washed his shirt in holy water, she sewed a red ribbon in his belt, and she put an acorn in his pocket.

It made no difference at all. Nicola continued to spend as much time as he could diving and swimming underwater, deep down among the coral reefs. He still brought back stories of all the wonderful things to be seen at the bottom of the sea. The only consolation his mother had was that she had at least proved that his strange ways and strange habits were not the work of the Devil.

Nicola eventually became famous all over the island for his skill at diving. People called him Nicola Pesce, Nicola the Fish, because he seemed to be so much more at home under the water than on the surface of the earth. Even the Emperor Frederick II of Sicily heard about him, with the result that when he came on a visit to Messina he ordered the youth to be brought before him. So Nicola went to the palace, and saw the Emperor sitting on his throne, and beside the Emperor was the Emperor's daughter, a golden-haired, blue-eyed maiden of seventeen.

Nicola bowed low before the Emperor, and before the Princess, and even when the Emperor spoke to him he found it hard to keep his eyes from dwelling on the maiden's face. She was very fair.

'Is it true,' Frederick asked him, 'that you can dive

deeper and stay under water longer than any other man in the world?'

'I do not know, Your Majesty, for I do not know what others can do.'

'Let us find out then,' said the Emperor. He ordered that they should all go on board the imperial barge, and that the ship should move out into deep water. Then he took up a golden cup and threw it far over the side of the ship. 'Bring me back my cup,' he said to Nicola.

Nicola dived in and recovered the cup without any difficulty. While he was under the water he also broke off a tiny piece of the most beautiful coral he could find, deep red, like a jewel. Then he came up to the surface, climbed aboard the barge, and presented the cup to the Emperor and the coral to the Princess.

'Keep the cup as a souvenir,' Frederick told him. 'Now bring me back my sword,' and he threw his heavy sword, still in the scabbard, overboard. Nicola dived in again and quickly recovered the sword.

'Well done,' said Frederick, 'But there are other divers who might have done the same. Now you must do something more difficult for me.'

'I will try, whatever it is,' said Nicola.

The Emperor then explained to him that no one had been able to find out what the foundations of the island of Sicily were; whether it stood on solid rock, whether it was supported by pillars, or whether it simply floated on the surface of the water. 'I want you to swim all the way around the island,' he said. 'From Messina past Palermo, past Castellamare, past Terranova, past Syracuse and Catania, and so back again to Messina.'

'The distance is great,' said Nicola. (It is in fact some five hundred miles or more.)

'I know,' said the Emperor. 'Take your time, resting whenever you like. But do not return until you have circled the whole of the island and discovered what lies beneath it.'

Nicola looked at the Emperor. He looked at the Princess. 'Wait for me,' he said, and the Princess knew that he was speaking to her. Then he dived overboard again.

The days and the weeks went by and the weeks became months. It had been spring when the Emperor ordered Nicola to swim round Sicily, and it was early autumn before the swimmer returned from his circuit of the island. Frederick received him again on board the imperial barge, with the Princess at his side.

'Your Majesty,' said Nicola, 'the island of Sicily rests on three huge granite columns, whose foundations lie deep in the ocean bed. These columns are solid rock, stronger than the mountains above us. But I must tell you that one of the columns, the one which stands

People called him Nicola Pesce, Nicola the Fish.

between Catania and Messina, is nevertheless in danger of being destroyed.'

'Destroyed by what?' the Emperor asked suspiciously.

'Destroyed by fire,' said Nicola. 'A great fire is smouldering at the base of the column, slowly eating away the stone. All the seaweed and the grasses in that region are already dead. No fish dares swim within a mile of it.'

Frederick looked at him doubtfully. 'How can a fire be burning under the sea?' he said. 'Surely the waters would have put it out.'

'The fire is too strong,' said Nicola. 'The water does keep it from spreading, but it cannot keep it from eating away at the base of the column itself.'

The Emperor remained unconvinced. 'If what you say is true,' he said, 'dive down again and bring me a sample of this fire that burns at the bottom of the sea.'

Nicola looked at the Emperor, and he looked at the Princess. 'Your Majesty,' he said, 'were I Saint Joseph himself, it would be impossible to bring you fire. How am I to get near enough to the flames; how am I to carry them?'

'That is up to you,' replied the Emperor, who was used to getting his own way in everything.

Then the Princess spoke for the first time, speaking to her father. 'It is true, what the young man says,' she told him. 'How is a man to carry flame?'

The Emperor would not listen to her any more than he would listen to Nicola. He insisted on having proof that a fire was actually burning in the depths of the sea. So Nicola dived overboard again, down, down, down towards the base of the granite column that stands between Messina and Catania. As he drew near it the cool green waters gradually grew warmer and warmer, and he could see a red glow and a cloud of smoke in front of him. He swam on and on until the water was so hot that he could hardly bear it. Then he closed his eyes and dived towards the fire, trying to catch some of the flame in his hands.

It was all in vain. He seized one flame after another, but each one slipped out of his hands, and he had nothing to show for it except that his hands were badly burned. Finally he gave up the attempt and floated slowly back to the surface of the water; there, too exhausted even to swim, he let the boatmen pull him up on to the imperial barge.

As soon as he had recovered his breath Nicola appeared before the Emperor again. 'Your Majesty,' he said, 'no man can capture flame. But I have brought you proof of the fire which burns at the base of the great granite pillar beneath us.' And he held up his hands, blistered and burnt by the fire.

Emperor Frederick nodded his head. 'I believe you,' he said. 'It is clear that there must be a great fire burning underneath us. But if that is so then the island of Sicily itself is in great danger, for if one of the three pillars falls the whole island will sink below the surface of the water, and all its people will be lost.'

'It is so, Your Majesty.'

The Emperor was silent for a few moments, staring down at the deck of the ship, and no one else dared speak. At last he turned back to Nicola. 'You must find out more about this danger,' he told him. 'Dive down just once again and discover the source of the fire, and how soon the pillar will crumble, and what we can do to put out the flames.'

Nicola looked at the Emperor. He looked at the Princess. 'Your Majesty,' he said, 'it is impossible.'

'Are you afraid?' demanded Frederick.

'No, I am not afraid,' Nicola told him, 'but if I dive down into the fire again I will never come back.'

'It is true, what the young man says,' the Princess repeated sadly. 'If he goes down again he will not come back.'

'Nonsense,' said the Emperor. 'If he can dive twice he can dive three times.' He pointed out to them how important it was to determine the cause of the fire, and whether the granite pillar could still be saved, or whether they would have to evacuate the entire population of Sicily to the mainland.

'Very well,' said Nicola. 'If that is what you want. A man can only die once, and it is just as well for me to die where I have lived so much of my life – under the waters of the sea. Only let me go home first and say farewell to my mother and my father.'

He went home and told his family what had happened. His mother wept when she heard the story, and his father and his brothers found it hard to keep from weeping too, but at the same time they tried to cheer him up; they told him that they were sure he would come back safely from under the sea, and that they would all be waiting to welcome him when he did. Nicola knew better. He walked through the garden for the last time, and along the neighbouring shore, where fishing nets were spread out on the shore to dry and little fishing boats were visible far on the horizon. He looked across to the mainland, only a giant's step away, for the last time.

When he had said farewell to everything he loved at

home he went aboard the Emperor's barge for the last time. 'I am ready to dive again,' he told the Emperor Frederick. Then he looked at the golden-haired, blue-eyed Princess, and she returned his look. 'Do not wait for me,' he said, and he dived quickly overboard.

Weeks and months passed, but Nicola never returned. The Princess did not give up hope for a long time. She would wander every day along the seashore a little south of Messina, in the direction of Catania, holding in her hand the beautiful, bright piece of coral which Nicola had brought her the very first time he dived overboard for the Emperor, watching and waiting for some sign of him.

One day as she stood on the sand looking out to sea she noticed a little whirlpool of seaweed quite close to the shore, a swirling mass of silvery weed and foam. She watched it for a while and as she watched it she heard a voice, seeming to come from the seaweed itself, which she knew was the voice of Nicola.

'Do not wait for me, beautiful Princess,' it said; 'Do not grieve. For I shall never return.'

'What happened?' she said softly.

'I dived down and down and down,' said the voice, 'and when I reached the base of the pillar I could see that it was much worse. The flame was burning brighter than before, and the column itself was swaying a little. I could not let Sicily fall. So I dived into the heart of the flame, and put my shoulder to the pillar and held it firm, and there I must stay for ever.'

'But you must be in agony from the flames!' she cried.

'Oh no,' said the voice. 'Oh no. The fire rages outside but the fire here in the very centre of the blaze does not burn. There is no pain. It is only that I must stay for ever, or at least until the end of the world we know.'

The whirlpool swirled on its way, and the voice was silent. The melancholy Princess stayed where she was for a long time, looking out to sea, but she knew that she could not stay there for ever. Nor could she wait for Nicola, who would not return.

A few years later the Princess agreed to marry a man of her father's choice. She loved her husband, and she loved her children. But she never forgot the dark-haired youth who had dived so often from the deck of her father's imperial barge and who had once brought her a sprig of coral from the depths of the sea. Whenever she looked out to sea she thought of him. Whenever she saw the sea-birds flying, or seaweed drifting, she remembered him. Whenever she sailed anywhere on any ship, large or small, she would look far, far down into the water and know that somewhere in the depths of the sea below her Nicola was supporting the great granite pillar standing between Messina and Catania, and that therefore Sicily was safe from harm.

That was seven hundred years ago, and more. But as far as anyone knows Nicola Pesce is still there, still upholding his native island.

SEVEN

Pietro Bailliardo

ONE DAY A Roman scholar whose name was Pietro Bailliardo was looking at books in a bookshop when he came across a small volume on witchcraft and devils. At first he looked at it without much interest, but as he turned the pages he suddenly realized that it provided all the necessary diagrams, words and formulas to enable the reader to call up any number of devils and make them do whatever he wanted them to do. Pietro did not really believe that the spells would work. Nevertheless he bought the book, took it home with him, and promptly tried out some of the formulas described there. Sure enough, the devils appeared, ready to do his bidding.

After that Pietro Bailliardo lived a very comfortable and easy life. He never needed to work, he never needed to study, he never needed to do anything for himself. The devils did it all. If he wanted a house or a carriage, or horses, they provided these for him; if he wanted food, they brought it to him; if he wanted to do well in his examinations, they made the teachers give him the best marks of all, even though he had done no work. If he wanted to play tricks on his schoolmates, or take revenge on someone he did not like, he simply called on one of the devils to arrange it for him.

There was one young girl for instance whom Pietro tried to make love to, who would have nothing to do with him. So what did he do but get his devils to carry the poor girl away to the top of a high hill outside Rome and leave her there, with a circle of fire burning around her, so that it was a long time before anyone could get near enough to rescue her. After this incident the girl's family, and a number of other people who had also suffered from his mischievous magic, accused Pietro of witchcraft and he was arrested and thrown into prison. Next morning, when the jailer came by to make sure that all the prisoners were in their places he found that Pietro had vanished; the head of a donkey was lying in the bed where he should have been.

Pietro was arrested again soon after this, on another charge of witchcraft. This time the locks and bolts on the prison gates were strengthened, and the guards doubled, so that he would have no chance of escaping. But as soon as the jailer had gone Pietro took a piece of charcoal out of his pocket and drew a picture of a boat on the white walls of the prison cell. It was a large and very real looking boat. In fact it was so real that when it was finished Pietro stepped right into it.

'Come on,' he said to his fellow-prisoners. 'We might as well get out of here!'

Although most of the prisoners were too frightened to follow, three or four crowded into the boat beside him. Pietro took up the oars, gave a few strokes, and they found themselves drifting downstream on the River Tiber, just near Rome.

All this time Pietro knew perfectly well that by employing these spells and calling on the devils to serve him, he must have given his soul up to the Devil. It did not worry him very much at first. Then one fine day he noticed a well-dressed man following him on the street and suddenly, instinctively, and to his horror realized that this man was the Devil himself. At the same time he realized that, since he was able to see and recognize him, the Devil had undoubtedly come to collect his, Pietro's soul.

Fortunately, Pietro was too quick for the enemy. He ran into the nearest church he could find, where of course the Devil could not follow him, and stayed there all day. He said his prayers over and over again, all day. Yet even as he said them, he knew that he could not very well expect these last-minute prayers to get rid of the Devil for him.

When night fell the priest came and asked him to leave, because they had to close the church for the night. Pietro went as far as the door, and looked out, and there was the Devil – with a jaunty cap on his head and a smile on his lips – still waiting for him just beyond the steps of the church. He ran back in again and explained to the priest that he dared not leave the church, his soul being in danger.

The priest took him to see the Abbot, to whom he told his story.

'Well,' said the Abbot, 'I do not see how your soul can be saved. But let us go to the Grand Inquisitor, at the Palace of the Inquisition, and see what he has to say about it.'

'I cannot leave the church,' Pietro explained again. 'The Devil is waiting just outside.'

'Oh yes, you can,' said the Abbot; 'We will just take

these with us.' He gathered up several of the most holy relics in the church, including one or two small bones of different Saints, and carried these in his right hand, holding Pietro firmly with his left. Thus protected, they stepped into the Abbot's carriage. When the Devil saw Pietro riding away with the Abbot, and realized that

It was as if a storm had struck the city.

for the time being he could not get anywhere near him, he flew into such a rage that it was as if a storm had struck the city, with thunder, lightning and high winds. But there was nothing he could do to harm the two men; they rode on to the Palace of the Inquisition and went in to see the Grand Inquisitor.

Pietro confessed his crimes to the Inquisitor, explaining how the Devil was already close on his heels and was in fact waiting just outside the church for him. The Inquisitor looked grave. 'I will do the best I can for you,' he said, 'but you have left your repentance rather late.' Then he looked sternly at Pietro – 'You do genuinely repent these sins you have confessed?' he asked him. 'You do regret the evil life you have been leading?'

'I do,' said Pietro. And he meant it.

'Well then, the first thing for you to do is to do penance by making pilgrimages to two of the most holy, and most distant, churches in the Christian world. When you have done that, come back to me and ask for absolution, and by that time I may be able to save your soul.'

'That is very kind of you,' said Pietro. 'Which are the churches I must visit?'

'That of Saint James the Apostle, at Compostella,' said the Inquisitor, 'and that of the Holy Sepulchre at Jerusalem.'

'Very well,' said the repentant sinner. 'I suppose, since this sort of thing is your business, you have thought of a way to keep the Devil from molesting me while I do this penance?'

'Oh yes.' The Inquisitor gave him a tiny little box, containing a few hairs from the head of one of the earliest Christian Saints. 'Just keep this with you. But remember,' he added, 'it will not keep you safe for ever; only until you have made your pilgrimage.'

So Pietro went home, safe from the Devil, and sat down and thought about how best to carry out his pilgrimages. Among his books he found a map of the world, in which he could locate the two churches. He saw that the Church of Santiago, or Saint James, at Compostella was a good thousand miles away from Rome, to the west, in the very furthest north-west corner of Spain. The Church of the Holy Sepulchre in Jerusalem was about fifteen hundred miles away from Rome in almost exactly the opposite direction, south of east.

'Two thousand miles there and back to Compostella, and three thousand there and back to Jerusalem,' he said to himself. 'Good heavens! It will take me years to travel that on foot, or even on horseback.'

Unfortunately Pietro had been so long in the habit of opening his little book on witchcraft whenever he needed help that, quite without thinking, he picked it up now. 'I wonder,' he mused, 'if there is not some easier way of travelling.'

The next thing he knew he was surrounded by half a dozen junior devils. (You might have thought that the relic, the little box with the Saint's hair, which Pietro carried, would have kept the devils away – but no. That only ensured that the Devil himself could not take Pietro's soul.)

'I can travel as fast as the wind,' one of the devils told him.

'Well now, that is much better,' said Pietro. 'But even the wind would take several days to get to Compostella, and all the way back to Jerusalem.'

Then another devil spoke up. 'I can travel as fast as sound,' he said.

'I don't really know how fast sound travels,' said Pietro. 'But I suppose it must be faster than the wind.'

'It is,' said a third devil, 'but it is nothing like as fast as thought. Thought is the quickest thing in the world. And I can travel as quickly as thought.'

'That's wonderful!' cried Pietro, never stopping to think that being transported by devils was not a very good way to make a pilgrimage. 'You can take me to both these churches tonight, and we will be back here by tomorrow morning.'

He climbed on the Devil's back, and they set off at once. They flew due west out across the Mediterranean Sea, over the island of Corsica, and then across the whole great width of the Spanish Peninsula, but they flew so fast that Pietro scarcely had time to catch his breath before they were coming down on the outskirts of Compostella. There before them was the great Cathedral of Saint James.

'Wait for me here,' said Pietro, and he went on alone to join a throng of pilgrims who were moving slowly towards the Cathedral for the evening prayers. There were a great many of them, for this was one of the most holy churches in all Christendom, being believed to contain the actual bones of Saint James the Apostle. Legend told how when Saint James had died, far away in Palestine, his disciples had placed his body in a ship, with sails ready set, and allowed it to drift out to sea so that the great Apostle might choose his own resting-place. The miracle was that the very next day the boat had reached the coast of north-west Spain, which is nearer fifteen hundred than a thousand miles by sea. Some people said that the boat in which the Saint travelled was made of marble, which was even more miraculous, and that an enormous stone still standing at Compostella was the remains of the magic vessel.

Be that as it may, the Cathedral of Santiago de

Compostella became so famous that it was the goal of almost every medieval pilgrim. Pietro was much impressed by all this. He lit a candle at the shrine of the Saint. He made offerings for the Church, for the poor, and for the souls of the dead. He also bought a talisman in the form of a scallop shell, which is sacred to Saint James, to prove that he had actually visited the holy shrine. Then he went back and found his devil again.

'Very well,' he said. 'Let us be on our way to Jerusalem.

They set off again, as fast as before. They flew across Spain for the second time, across the Mediterranean, over Corsica and Sardinia. They did not stop in Italy at all this time but flew straight on across the peninsula, south of Rome, and on again across the eastern Mediterranean, above Greece and Crete, until at last they came to the Holy Land.

It was dark by this time, and all they could see were a few scattered lights when they passed over a city or a town. Once or twice the devil looked back and said, wonderingly, 'Why should a devil be carrying anyone to the Holy Land?' but Pietro simply kicked him and retorted that it was none of his business. 'You just do as you are told,' he said, and they flew on.

They circled high over the hills of Palestine and came down to land inside the walls of ancient Jerusalem, the most sacred city in the Christian world. There stood the great Church of the Holy Sepulchre. The doors of the church were still open, although it was already midnight, and a number of worshippers were gathered here and there inside, praying. Pietro made his way around the entire church, stopping often to pray and to light a candle, until at last he crawled inside the little shrine in the centre of the building which was the actual grave where the body of Christ was laid. There too he said his prayers.

Finally he bought a talisman in the form of a little wooden cross, which had been blessed by a Pope of long ago. Well satisfied with himself, he went back to where the devil was waiting and ordered him to fly back to Rome.

Next morning Pietro presented himself before the Grand Inquisitor.

'I have made my pilgrimages,' he said. 'I have lit a candle at the altar of Santiago de Compostella, and here is the scallop shell I brought back from there. I have lit candles at the Church of the Holy Sepulchre, and here is the holy cross I brought from there.'

The Grand Inquisitor stared at him in horror. He knew without asking that Pietro had had the help of devils, for there was no other means by which he could have travelled five thousand miles in a single night.

'There is nothing more I can do for you,' he said, shaking his head sadly. 'It is obvious that you are in league with the Devil. Neither I nor anyone else on this earth can give you absolution.'

Then Pietro realized what he had done. He understood that the reason for his pilgrimage had been that he should make the long, long journey to the different shrines, suffering hardship on the way, and not that he should use whatever means he could find to travel there and back as quickly and as comfortably as possible. 'Oh dear,' he thought to himself. 'Now it is too late. The Devil will be waiting outside again.'

He went slowly down the long corridor away from the office of the Grand Inquisitor. But he did not leave the Palace of the Inquisition. 'If no one on earth can give me absolution,' he thought, 'I must find it elsewhere.'

He went into the little chapel just inside the entrance of the palace, and knelt before the crucifix there. 'I swear that I will not leave here,' he said, 'until I am either dead, or forgiven.'

He prayed there for a long time. After that he picked up a stone and began beating himself on the head and breast until the blood flowed from his wounds, and finally he fainted on the ground in front of the Cross. Then the Lord looked down. He could see, as the Grand Inquisitor could not, that Pietro, in spite of his foolishness and his past sins, was truly penitent. He nodded His head slowly on the Cross.

'I forgive you,' He said.

So Pietro Bailliardo was saved. He went home and burned the book on witchcraft, page by page. The Devil never came near him again, he never again called on the junior devils for help, and he died, a long time later, in peace.

EIGHT

Stupid Peruonto

AN ELDERLY peasant woman called Ceccarella lived on the outskirts of a royal city in one of the kingdoms of southern Italy, making her living as best she could. She had only one son, who, to her great disappointment, grew up to be an ugly, stupid and lazy youth. She had to admit that he was also good-tempered, kind-hearted and cheerful. But that was very little consolation to her when she tried to get him to help her around the house, or to go out and earn a living for himself. Whenever his mother asked him to do any work, Peruonto, for that was his name, would make no answer but just go on cheerfully sitting in the sun and doing nothing. Even when he did occasionally try to help her he usually made things worse; he was so clumsy and inefficient.

One day Ceccarella asked Peruonto to collect a bundle of firewood for her. She asked him once, and she asked him twice, and finally the third time she asked him he heard what she was saying and agreed to go and fetch the wood. He took his axe and set off for the forest nearby, walking slowly, for it was a beautiful, warm summer's day and he was in no hurry to get to work.

In order to reach the forest he had to cross a broad meadow. And there in the meadow he came upon three youths who were lying asleep. When Peruonto saw this he thought to himself, in his kindly, stupid way, that the youths must be very uncomfortable lying there in the hot sun on such a hot day and that they would be much happier if only they had some shade to cover them. So he took his axe, cut a great pile of branches from an oak tree nearby and in a very short time had built a shelter of green oak boughs which shaded the three sleepers from the sun. He enjoyed doing this; it was much more fun than chopping firewood.

When he had finished the shelter he set off again, still slowly, for the forest. But just then the three youths woke up and, seeing what had happened, called him back. 'Why did you build this roof to shelter us, sleeping, from the sun?' they asked him.

'Because I thought you looked hot and uncomfortable and would be better off in the shade,' Peruonto told them.

When they heard this the three youths, who happened to be the three sons of a fairy, were so grateful that they bestowed on Peruonto the power to have whatever he wanted, whenever he wanted it. He had only to make a wish and it would be fulfilled.

Someone else would probably have tried out this power immediately, and made his fortune. But Peru-onto was so stupid that it never occurred to him to wish for anything. He thanked the three youths and went on his way, and when he reached the forest he started chopping wood to take home to his mother. He chopped and chopped and chopped away. When he finally stopped and bound all the wood he had cut into a single faggot, the bundle was so enormous that he could not possibly have carried it home.

He sat down on top of the faggot. 'How stupid I am,' he said to himself. 'This faggot is twice as big as I am. I can't even lift it. How I wish things were the other way round, and it would carry me home instead of my having to carry it home.'

The next thing he knew was that the faggot rose a few feet above the ground. Then, like a horse, it galloped away so quickly that it was all Peruonto could do to hold on to the branches.

The faggot, with Peruonto astride it, galloped from the forest to the meadow, across the meadow to the city and through the city from one side to the other, for the village where Ceccarella lived was on the far side of the city. As they rode through the city streets they passed by the palace where the King lived. And as they passed the palace the King's daughter, Vastolla, happened to be looking out of the window and saw Peruonto riding by on his great bundle of wood. She thought this was the funniest thing she had ever seen; she laughed and laughed and called her handmaidens to look out of the window at the absurd sight of a man who had only a faggot for a horse, and all the handmaidens laughed with her.

Peruonto looked up at the window and saw the laughing Princess. 'What is so funny about this?' he demanded indignantly. 'Have you nothing better to do than make fun of people? I wish I could be your husband some day; then you would soon stop laughing at me.'

It still did not occur to him that anything he wished would come true. Nor did he realize that if he wanted to marry the Princess all he had to do was to wish for the faggot to stop, and it would stop, and to wish that

She saw Peruonto riding by on his great bundle of wood.

the Princess would marry him, and she would marry him. Instead the faggot went galloping on its way and he was carried out of sight of the palace even while he was still speaking, so that he thought no more about it.

But a spell fell upon the Princess. She no longer laughed with her handmaidens, nor sang songs, nor danced, nor walked in the palace gardens. She simply sat by her window and sighed and sighed. Seeing her so melancholy all day long, her father the King decided that it was time she should be married, and he asked her which one of the princes of the neighbouring kingdoms she would like to have as her husband. The Princess only sighed more deeply and said that she must marry a young man whom she had seen riding by the palace one day on a faggot of wood, and that she could marry no one else. The King first begged and then ordered her to change her mind, threatening to lock her up in a dungeon unless she agreed to marry one of the princes he had suggested, but it was all in vain. To make matters worse, she did not even know the name of the youth she was determined to marry.

This was the first time that anyone had ever refused to obey the King's command. He was so angry that he threatened to disown Vastolla, or send her into exile. But his councillors dissuaded him. 'She is your only daughter, and you have no son,' they reminded him; 'Who then is to inherit your kingdom? Let us at least find this youth she has fallen in love with. He may well be a prince in disguise, or a wealthy merchant, or a nobleman with great estates; you may be glad to have him for a son-in-law, once we can find him.'

'How do you expect to find him?' demanded the King.

'Let us give a banquet for all the eligible young men in the country,' the councillors suggested. 'Surely the Princess will be able to recognize her lover among them.'

The King did as they advised him. He summoned nobles, princes, merchants, and other eligible young men from every part of the country to come to the palace one evening for a great feast. He told Vastolla that she could make her choice among them. Whereupon the Princess looked them all over and said that the man she must marry was not to be found among these.

The King was so angry that he now threatened to have his ungrateful daughter put to death at once. But again his councillors dissuaded him.

'You must make one last effort to satisfy the Princess,' they told him. 'You must hold another banquet and invite all the unmarried youths of the city, whoever they may be, the fishermen and the tailors, the comb-sellers and the bricklayers, the brewers and the bakers and the greengrocers. Who knows where the Princess's fancy may have led her, or on what humble, handsome and deserving youth her choice may have fallen?'

'Do you think I would let my daughter marry a baker or a greengrocer?' the King protested. Nevertheless, he did as he was told, and issued a proclamation inviting all youths of marriageable age to come to the palace. When Ceccarella heard that a feast was to be held at the palace for the common youths of the city and the neighbouring villages, she insisted that Peruonto must go.

'At least you will get a good meal,' she said.

So Peruonto put on his best suit, which was none too good, combed his hair, and off he went to the palace on foot. It never occurred to him to wish for a new suit, or a horse to ride. No sooner had he entered the great hall of the palace, however, than Vastolla knew him for the youth whom she had seen riding the faggot and cried out that this was the man she would marry.

'What!' exclaimed the King, staring at Peruonto. 'Do

'What! Do you mean to marry this lout.'

you mean to marry this lout, this ugly, dull-witted youth without even a decent suit to his name?'

'I do,' said the Princess.

The King realized that Peruonto must have cast some manner of spell over his beautiful daughter, or Vastolla would never have fallen in love with him. But this did not make him any less angry. He lost his temper completely.

'Very well,' he said. 'Marry him you shall, this very day. But you will not live to enjoy each other's company for long.' He gave orders that the wedding should take place at once, and that as soon as the wedding ceremony was over the bride and groom should be sealed up in a large cask together, and the cask thrown into the sea.

No one dared disobey the King. The cask was prepared, Peruonto and Vastolla were shut up inside it, the lid was firmly nailed down and four strong men dragged it down to the sea and hurled it as far out into the waves as they could. The tide soon swept it beyond sight of land.

Before the cask was sealed Vastolla's maids had managed to hide a quantity of dried figs and raisins inside it so that the couple would not starve. 'But what good is that?' Vastolla thought bitterly as they drifted further and further out to sea, tossed hither and thither by the waves. 'We will suffocate here; if we do not suffocate, we will drown; if we do not drown, we will starve to death as soon as we have eaten the last of the figs and the raisins.' And she wept as though her heart would break.

'Why are you weeping?' asked Peruonto, who was so slow-witted that it had not yet occurred to him that they were in any danger.

'You fool!' she said, 'I am weeping because we will both very soon be dead. Here we are in the middle of the ocean, with no one to save us; no ship, no shore, no friendly fisherman or mariner to come to our rescue.'

'If you want a ship, I could wish for one,' said Peruonto. 'It's a very strange thing, but I am beginning to think that those three young men I met in the meadow meant what they said. Whatever I wish for seems to happen.'

'If that is so, what on earth are we waiting for?' asked the astonished Princess. 'Quickly now, wish for the lid of this horrible cask to be opened, and then wish for a well-fitted ship to come to our rescue.'

'There is no hurry,' said Peruonto, who liked to take his time about things. 'Let us have something to eat first. I like raisins and figs, and it seems a pity to waste them.'

Vastolla impatiently fed him with figs and raisins until he could eat no more. Then he made his wishes. The lid of the cask promptly flew open, and there in front of them was a beautiful ship, with tall white sails, and a complete crew: oarsmen, stewards, cooks, servants and even a lady's maid for the Princess. All they had to do was climb aboard.

For several months they lived happily on the ship, sailing the far seas. But at length Vastolla began to long for dry land, for gardens and for forests and for the life she had known in her father's palace. 'Surely we do not want to spend our whole life at sea?' she said to Peruonto. 'Why not wish for a palace and a kingdom of our own?'

'I suppose we might as well,' said Peruonto. 'But there is no hurry. I am happy here. Let us have just a few more raisins and figs, and then I will see what I can do.'

When he had eaten his fill of the figs and the raisins, he made his wish. There on the shore ahead of them appeared a palace, with gardens and orchards and farms beyond it; it was beautifully furnished and with an entire staff waiting to serve them. So they went ashore and lived in the palace with everything in the world they both wanted.

Or almost everything. One day the Princess came to her husband, bringing a large bowl of figs and raisins. 'Will you make one more wish for me?' she asked.

'Why not?' said Peruonto. 'What is it you would like.'

'Well,' said Vastolla, rather nervously. 'I do love you as you are. I will always love you. But it would be nice if you were a little better-looking and a little more clever.'

To her surprise, Peruonto was not in the least annoyed. 'It is all the same to me,' he said, 'if it will make you happy.'

He ate a good many raisins and figs, until he was in the right mood. Then he wished. The next thing he knew he was as handsome as any prince, and a good deal more clever than most. After that, he did not need Vastolla's urging to use his magic powers; he used them whenever it would benefit the people of his newly-acquired kingdom, and occasionally even for his own amusement in getting things done around the castle. He saved his servants a great deal of work by wishing for things to happen which they would otherwise have had to do.

Meanwhile the old King, Vastolla's father, had never ceased to regret his cruelty towards his daughter and her ill-favoured husband. He spent as much time as he could away from his own palace, where he could not help thinking of Vastolla, and of her fate, and he often went on hunting trips into other parts of the country. On one such occasion he was caught by a snowstorm far from home and sought shelter at an impressive-looking castle nearby, which he had never seen before.

The King was received at the castle by two good-looking, fair-haired boys, who made him welcome and invited him to dine and spend the night. To his great surprise, there was no one else in sight. No maid-servants, no valet, no waiters. Everything in the castle apparently happened by magic. When it was time for dinner a table appeared beside him, with food and drink laid out upon it; as soon as he had finished eating it disappeared again. Throughout the evening he could hear the sound of music by a full orchestra coming to him from one corner of the great hall, but not a single musician was visible anywhere. When it was time to go to bed, a candle, carried by an invisible hand, led the way upstairs to his bedroom, where he found everything already prepared for his comfort.

Next morning he had scarcely opened his eyes when breakfast appeared beside him. A fresh suit of clothes had been laid out for him and a hot bath was ready in the bathroom. As soon as he was dressed he hurried downstairs to look for the two children he had seen the night before; he could scarcely wait to ask them about the invisible servants who had attended to his needs in such a mysterious way.

He found the children waiting for him, much amused by his perplexity in the face of these magical happenings. With the children was their mother. And what was his joy to discover that their mother was none other than his daughter Vastolla, whom he had thought drowned so many years before. She called her husband, and the King was even more astonished to discover that Peruonto, whom he had condemned to death because of his stupidity and ugliness, had become a handsome and exceptionally intelligent young man. The two fair-haired boys were his own grandchildren.

The King begged their forgiveness, which was readily granted, and then Vastolla told him how all this had come about. The King ruefully admitted his mistake.

'I called Peruonto stupid,' he said. 'But I was more stupid than he ever was. I should have known that if he could work one magic spell he could work another.'

After this reunion Vastolla and her husband and the two boys spent half of each year in their own magic castle and half of the year with the old King in his palace. Peruonto also invited his mother, Ceccarella, to come and live at the palace, where she was looked after for the rest of her life and lived in greater comfort than she had ever imagined.

The only trouble was that poor Ceccarella, who perhaps was not so very bright herself, could never be convinced that this handsome son-in-law of the King's, who had bestowed such good fortune upon her, was her own lost Peruonto.

'Nonsense,' she retorted whenever he tried to explain things to her. 'Don't I know my own son? It is all very kind of you to look after an old woman like me, and I am certainly grateful, but you don't need to pretend that you do it because I am your mother. Magic or no magic, that is quite impossible.'

Even when she died, many, many years later, Ceccarella was still saying to herself —

'That good-for-nothing Peruonto. I wonder whatever did become of him?'

NINE

La Cenerentola

FLORENCE, THE capital of the province of Tuscany, stands on the banks of the river Arno, with the hills of central Italy rising behind it, and the Florentines say that it is the most beautiful city in Italy – and therefore in the whole world. No other city, they say, has so many magnificent palaces, museums and churches, including the great Duomo, or Cathedral, that stands in the very centre of the city, with a Baptistery and Campanile, or bell tower, of equal beauty. No other city, they say, has given so many painters, sculptors and architects to Italy. Nor is any other city surrounded by groves of cypress and poplar trees, nor by gardens and fields where flowers grow wild in such abundance that the city is nicknamed 'La Città dei Fiori', the City of Flowers.

The Romans and the Venetians may dispute this claim, thinking their own ancient cities to be more beautiful, but no one denies that Florence is a great and lovely city. Many legends and fairy stories have been told about it, through the years and centuries. And sometimes a story which is well known in other parts of the world either had its origin in Florence, or has long since been adopted there.

In Florence for instance they tell the story of a Tuscan

merchant who once lived not far from there, and who had three daughters. He travelled far, both in Italy and across the sea, and often brought back presents for his three daughters. One day however he called the three girls together and told them that he was going away on a longer voyage than ever before, to more distant countries than he had yet visited.

'This time you may choose for yourselves what you would like me to bring you,' he said. 'Choose anything in the world you want, and I will find it for you.'

The eldest daughter promptly said that she would like a beautiful dress, all silk, and a bracelet and a necklace to wear with it. The second daughter said that she would like a shawl woven from gold thread, a hat with fine feathers, and a necklace as well. The third daughter, a quiet girl whom her sisters always made fun of and who was called Cenerentola – or, as we might say, Cinderella – because she liked to sit in a corner of the fireplace among the ashes, said nothing. She never did say very much. She was too shy, and anyway she was so busy thinking her own thoughts and dreaming her own dreams that she often did not hear what other people were saying to her.

'Well,' her father repeated, 'what shall I bring you from across the seas?'

'If you bring me anything,' she said at last, 'bring me a little bird.'

Her elder sisters laughed merrily when they heard this. 'You silly girl,' they mocked her. 'What can you do with a bird? When the Prince invites us all to the palace ball and we put on our new dresses and our new jewels, you will have nothing to wear.'

'That is as it may be,' said Cenerentola, 'but a little bird is the only thing I want.'

They all bade their father farewell, and just before he left the house she said to him again: 'Bring me a little bird. Do not forget, I beg you, for now I have set my heart upon it; if you do forget you may well find that you cannot reach home again.'

The merchant went on his way, across the hills and down to the coast, where he embarked on a great ship sailing from Venice. He reached the far country across the seas for which he was bound, and he bought many things there that he could trade or sell in Italy at a good profit. He bought an embroidered silk dress for his eldest daughter, and a bracelet and necklace; he bought a golden shawl and a feathered hat and a necklace for his second daughter. But he forgot the bird. In fact he never thought about the bird at all, for it seemed such an unlikely thing to ask for that he had not taken his youngest daughter's request very seriously.

Finally, when he had everything he wanted, he went on board the ship which was to carry him back to Venice. The sails were set, there was a fair wind, and the captain ordered the crew to cast off and put out to sea. To everyone's astonishment, nothing happened. The ship remained as close to the shore as though she were anchored there with a dozen heavy anchors.

The captain immediately realized that some magic influence must be at work. He called the passengers together on the deck.

'I feel sure that one of you has forgotten something,' he said. 'Some errand you were asked to do, some promise you made, has been neglected. The ship will not move until the errand has been done.'

Then the merchant suddenly remembered. 'The bird!' he cried; 'I promised my youngest daughter to bring her a bird, and I had completely forgotten it. Moreover she warned me that if I failed to find a bird for her my ship might not be able to reach home again.'

'If that is all, it is easily remedied,' said the captain. 'There is a garden nearby, over there beyond the trees, which is filled with the most beautiful birds you can imagine. They are quite tame. All you have to do is to catch one for your daughter, and then we will be on our way.'

The merchant, having borrowed a birdcage, made his way at once to the garden. He found that it was exactly as the captain had said. Birds of every colour were flitting from tree to tree, chirruping to each other, and he had scarcely opened the door of his cage before a small green bird flew into it, settled down on the perch and began to preen its feathers. The merchant hastily shut the cage and returned to his ship. Thereupon its sails at once filled with the breeze, the ship moved gracefuly out to sea, and the captain set his course for Venice.

The three girls were delighted with their presents. The eldest daughter and the second daughter wasted no time in trying on their dresses and shawls and jewels, admiring themselves before the mirror. The youngest daughter carried the little bird, which she called Verdeliò, off to her own room, where she petted it and played with it and talked to it all day long.

Soon after the merchant's return home the Prince of that city anounced that he would give three balls on three successive evenings. The merchant, who was well known at the palace and had often been of service to the Prince during his travels, was invited to attend, with his three daughters. You can well imagine the excitement that this invitation caused in the household! For at least a week before the first ball was to take place the two elder sisters were busy trying on their ball-gowns, their shawls, their slippers, deciding which jewellery to wear, and doing their hair in a dozen different styles before they could make up their minds

The ship moved gracefully out to sea.

which one they liked best. All this time Cenerentola sat in her favourite corner beside the chimney, watching them.

'Aren't you coming to the ball?' her sisters asked her over and over again, when they were not studying their own reflections in the mirror. 'We were all three invited; we can all three go.'

Cenerentola sat in her favourite corner beside the chimney, watching them.

'Leave me alone,' she said. 'Why should I go to the ball? Even if I did want to go, I have nothing to wear.'

'See how foolish you were not to ask father to bring you back a dress?' the sisters laughed at her. 'You can hardly expect your little bird to provide you with a ball-gown.'

So on the night of the first ball the merchant and his two older daughters set off alone for the palace. Cenerentola watched them go. Then she went up to her own room, where the little bird was singing. 'O Bird Verdeliò,' she said, 'O Bird Verdeliò, make me more beautiful than I am, so that I may go to the ball.'

No sooner had she spoken than she found herself dressed in a ball-gown of sea-green silk, with diamonds woven through it. She was wearing a crown, and silver slippers, and her face was so radiantly beautiful that no one would have recognized the quiet little girl who had sat by the fire all day. Moreover a carriage was waiting for her outside the house, with coachman and horses, while inside the carriage were two purses filled with gold coins.

Cenerentola was so much more beautiful than anyone else at the ball that when she entered the palace everyone stopped dancing to look at her. Even the music stopped; the musicians put their instruments down and stared at the newcomer. The Prince took her by the hand and led her into the ballroom, where he danced with her over and over again through the whole evening. He asked her what her name was, who her parents were, where she lived, but she would not answer a single one of his questions. All she would do was to promise him that she would come back again on the following night.

Late in the evening she happened to be standing near her eldest sister, who, needless to say, did not recognize her. The younger sister drew out her handkerchief and as she did so the beautiful bracelet she was wearing slipped off her wrist and fell to the floor. Her sister picked it up and handed it back to Cenerentola, but the girl shook her head. 'Keep it,' she said. 'You are welcome to it.'

Then she stepped quickly into her carriage and was driven away before anyone at the ball noticed that she had gone. As she drove out of the palace gate however half a dozen servants, whom the Prince had ordered to follow her and find out where she lived, ran after the carriage. When Cenerentola realized what was happening she picked up the two bags of money she had found lying in the carriage and scattered the coins on the ground behind her, one bag on either side. Seeing all this gold, the servants naturally stopped to pick it up, while Cenerentola rode on and was soon out of their sight. There was nothing the poor wretches could do except go back and explain to the Prince what had happened. The Prince was so angry he thought of having them beheaded then and there, but he relented and agreed to let them lie in wait for the beautiful stranger again on the following night; he warned them that this time they must not be led astray by gold or any other treasure.

Cenerentola meanwhile hurried up to her own room. 'O Bird Verdeliò,' she cried, 'O Bird Verdeliò, make me uglier than I am.' Immediately she was dressed in rags again, with her hair dishevelled, and her face dark, and she went and sat by the chimneyplace until her father and her sisters came home.

'Oh Cenerentola,' they told her, 'You should have come to the ball. The palace was so bright, and the Prince so handsome, and there was a beautiful stranger there whom no one knew, and the Prince danced with her all night. And look' – the elder sister held out her bracelet – 'the stranger dropped this; I picked it up, and she bade me keep it. If only you had been there you might have had something too.'

'Leave me alone,' she said. 'What do I want with a bracelet?'

On the folowing evening the two older sisters again tried to persuade Cenerentola to go to the ball with them, and again she told them to go away and leave her alone. Nevertheless as soon as they had gone she went to her own room and cried out – 'O Bird Verdeliò, O Bird Verdeliò, make me more beautiful than I am.'

Then she found herself dressed in a lovely red silk gown, like the sun, with golden slippers and a golden necklace and a golden scarf round her shoulders. The carriage was waiting for her outside. And in the carriage were two bags of sand.

That night again the Prince danced every dance with her, begging her to tell him who she was. 'My sisters call me Cenerentola,' she said at last. 'But that is not my name.'

'It is a pretty name,' he said.

Late in the evening she was standing near her second sister, who, needless to say, did not recognize her, when she put her hand up to her throat and her golden necklace fell to the ground. Her sister picked it up and would have given it back to her, but Cenerentola would not take it. 'Keep it,' she said. 'You are welcome to it.'

Soon afterwards she stepped into her carriage and

drove quickly away, but not so quickly that she was not followed by the servants of the Prince. When she saw them running behind the carriage, and saw that she could not be rid of them, she opened the two bags of sand and threw the sand out behind her. The servants were completely blinded. By the time they could get their eyes open the carriage had disappeared again; there was nothing for it but to go back and tell the Prince what had happened. He was even angrier than he had been the night before. Nevertheless he agreed to let them have one more chance; on the following evening they must follow the beautiful stranger on horseback, he said, and if she escaped from them a third time he would have them all beheaded on the spot.

Meanwhile Cenerentola hurried home. 'O Bird Verdeliò,' she said, 'O Bird Verdeliò, make me uglier than I am.' And there she was, sitting in the ashes, when her father and her sisters came home.

'Oh Cenerentola,' they cried. 'You really must come to the ball tomorrow night. The beautiful stranger was there again, in a red dress, and the Prince danced with her all night. And look' – the second sister held out her golden necklace – 'the stranger dropped this, I picked it up, and she bade me keep it. If you had been there you might have had something too.'

'Leave me alone,' said the girl. 'What do I want with a necklace?'

Try as they would, the older sisters could not persuade Cenerentola to come with them to the third and last ball on the following night. But as soon as their carriage was out of sight she whispered to her little bird again – 'O Bird Verdeliò, O Bird Verdeliò, make me more beautiful than I am.'

At once she found herself dressed in the most beautiful dress that anyone could imagine, with all the colours of heaven woven into it, and with the stars and the moon sprinkled like silver along the edge of her hem. She was wearing diamond slippers and a diamond crown. The carriage was waiting for her outside, as usual, and she stepped in and was driven to the ball. But this time she never stopped to think how she would escape if the Prince's servants followed her home.

Throughout the evening the Prince begged her to tell him who she was and where she lived, and still she refused. 'I shall find you somewhere, sooner or later,' he told her, 'and when I do we will be married; now that I have seen you there is no other girl in the world I could possibly marry.'

Late in the evening she was standing near her father, who, needless to say, did not recognize her, when she pulled out her handkerchief and a golden snuff-box fell from her pocket. He picked it up and would have given it back, but she refused to take it. 'Keep it,' she said. 'You are welcome to it.'

Then she stepped into her carriage and drove away. The Prince's servants followed her on horseback, and now she no longer had gold or sand or any other way of getting rid of them. Although her horses galloped and galloped as fast as they could, the servants were still close behind her when she reached her own house. There she jumped out of the carriage and ran inside in such a hurry that she dropped one of her diamond shoes in the street outside the gate of the house, and did not dare to stop and pick it up. The servants found the shoe, saw exactly which house the girl had disappeared into, and rode back to the Prince in triumph.

'We saw her run into the house with our own eyes,' they told him. 'We could not follow her because she had locked the gate behind her. But here is the slipper she dropped as she ran.'

'Well done,' said the Prince. 'I will go there tomorrow, and find my bride.'

Cenerentola meanwhile hurried to her room, crying as she ran, 'O Bird Verdeliò, O Bird Verdeliò, make me more ugly than I am! Quickly, quickly, for my sisters will soon be here.'

There was no answer. She called, and called again. Not until she had called four times, and was almost in despair, did the little bird come fluttering back to the cage. 'You foolish girl!' he said. 'What good will it do if I make you ugly, now that your secret has been discovered?'

Cenerentola sat down on her bed and wept. 'When the Prince finds out who I am, he will never marry me,' she said. 'How can he marry a girl who sits by the chimney all day, while her sisters make fun of her? Dear Bird Verdeliò, you must make me uglier than I am just once more, so that the Prince will not recognize me.'

Reluctantly, the bird agreed. By the time the merchant and his daughters came home she was sitting there as usual in her rags, her hair untidy, her face dirty. 'What a shame you did not come to the ball,' her father told her, 'for now you will never have another chance. And look' – he held out his golden snuff-box – 'the beautiful stranger who danced all night with the Prince dropped this, I picked it up, and she bade me keep it. If you had been there you might have had something too.'

'Leave me alone,' said the girl. 'What do I want with a snuff-box?'

Early next morning the royal carriage drew up at the gate of the merchant's house and the Prince stepped out. The merchant greeted him respectfully, with a deep bow, all the time wondering why on earth the Prince should come to see him.

'How many daughters do you have?' asked the Prince.

'Two daughters, Your Highness,' the merchant replied. He thought it was better not to mention Cenerentola because if the Prince wanted to see his daughters he would be ashamed to present such an untidy, ill-dressed girl to him. Sure enough, the next thing the Prince did was ask to be introduced to the two girls.

The eldest sister and the second sister tidied themselves as best they could, and hurried out to curtsey before the Prince. He looked at first one and then the other, and it did not seem to him that either of these could be the beautiful stranger he had fallen in love with. Nevertheless he took out the diamond slipper. 'Does this slipper fit either of your daughters?' he asked the merchant.

The eldest sister took the slipper and tried it on, and it was much too big for her. The second sister took the slipper and tried it on, and it was much too small for her. Then the Prince turned to the merchant again.

'Are you sure these are your only daughters?' he demanded. 'Is there no other maiden living in your house?'

The merchant hesitated, and knew that he must tell the truth. 'I have indeed a third daughter,' he said. 'But she never leaves the house. She will never wear a pretty dress or even comb her hair. She sits all day in the corner by the chimney, among the ashes, so that we laugh at her and call her Cenerentola.'

'Cenerentola!' cried the Prince. 'That is the very name of the girl I am seeking. Call your third daughter at once, that I may see her.'

The two sisters called and called and called, and Cenerentola refused to come. Her father called, and still she would not come. 'Leave me alone,' she said, and she sat in the corner and wept. Finally the little bird fluttered down and perched on her shoulder.

'There is nothing for it,' he said. 'You must go down and curtsey to the Prince.'

'O Bird Verdeliò,' she said, 'O Bird Verdeliò, in that case make me more beautiful than I am, so I shall stay beautiful the rest of my life.'

'Very well,' said the bird. 'Only promise that you will take me with you wherever you go.'

'I promise,' she said. The next moment she was dressed as she had been the night before, in the colours of heaven, with the stars and the moon on the hem of her dress. But she only had one shoe. She slipped the bird inside the bosom of her dress, and slowly limped down the stairs.

'Oh dear,' thought her father, when he heard her footsteps coming awkwardly towards them. 'She even walks like an old hag. Whatever will the Prince say when he sees her?'

The door opened and Cenerentola stood there in all her beauty. Her father and her sisters stared at her with their mouths open. The Prince fell on his knees before her and held out the diamond slipper, the mate to the one she was wearing on her other foot. She slipped it on, and no one could have any doubt whatever that she was the beautiful stranger who had appeared three times at the three balls.

'Will you marry me?' asked the Prince.

'Yes,' she said.

They stepped into the carriage together and rode back to the palace. They were married the very next day, after Cenerentola had sent word to her father and her sisters to come and join in the wedding celebration. As for the bird Verdeliò, he stayed with her all the rest of her life; he sat on his perch and sang and sang and sang with happiness.

TEN

The Cobbler

ONCE UPON A time there was a cobbler who lived in Genoa, on the west coast of Italy, and who was tired of cobbling. His father had been a cobbler before him and he had grown up in the trade of shoe-making, stitching and nailing and working in leather all his young life, until by the time he was twenty-five years old he decided he had had enough of it. 'I am much too clever to spend the rest of my life making and mending shoes for other people,' he said to himself. 'I will go out and see the world. Who knows? – I might even make my fortune, and perhaps marry a beautiful princess as well.'

The cobbler was in fact a very clever young man, and brave. But he knew perfectly well that a princess, and in fact almost anyone else, would laugh at the idea of a poor cobbler going out to seek adventure, for all the world as though he had been born a prince. He would have to pretend to be something else.

The first thing he did was to buy a large, round piece of cheese. He took the cheese home, put it on his table and left it there for several days without touching it. When he looked at it again it was, as he had hoped, all covered with flies and tiny cheese-mites. Then he took up the shoe he had been cobbling and brought it down on the cheese with one great bang, killing or wounding an enormous number of flies and mites. He counted these carefully and discovered that he had killed four hundred and wounded another five hundred.

Next he bought a soldier's uniform, a cocked hat, and a sword. He put these on, and left his home, and looked around him at the city of Genoa for the last time. Then he turned and walked inland over the hills. He walked and walked and walked, until at length he came to a great city, which was the capital of the province, and saw the King's castle standing on a hill above the city. He immediately made his way up to the castle, where he asked to see the King.

When he had gained admittance to the King's throne room he bowed deeply before the monarch, saying:

'Your Majesty, let me introduce myself. I am known as the Lord of the Flies, and indeed I am a great warrior. In the last battle I fought, only a few days ago, I left behind me on the battlefield four hundred killed and another five hundred wounded.'

The King looked at him with some surprise. 'You do not look so fierce a warrior to me,' he said, 'but appearances are often misleading. If it is indeed as you say, you can do me a great favour.'

'Your Majesty has only to command me. My sword and my life are yours.'

The King then explained to him that there was a giant living in the forest not far away who was the terror of the countryside. Scarcely a day passed that the giant did not carry off some innocent peasant, or his wife or his daughter, so that he could have a meal of human flesh. The King had sent knights, warriors, and princes to try and overthrow this giant but they had all failed – and several of them had lost their lives in the attempt.

'Nothing could be easier,' said the cobbler, although he was far from feeling as confident as he sounded. 'This is just the sort of adventure I am looking for. If I bring you the giant's head, may I marry your daughter?'

'You certainly may,' the King promised him.

The cobbler took his sword and set off at once towards the giant's castle in the woods. The sword was only for show; he knew perfectly well that it would be of no use against a giant. But he also took with him some cream cheese and some plaster-of-paris, and as he walked he rolled and rolled the cheese and the plaster-of-paris together in his hands until they hardened into a number of large balls, streaked in such a way that they looked exactly like marble. Marble was plentiful in this part of Italy, and anyone seeing the balls was sure to think that they really were made of marble.

When he came within sight of the castle he climbed up into the branches of a tall tree nearby, and sat down to wait. He did not have to wait long. Even before the sun had set he could hear the giant coming home. The earth groaned and shivered under his weight, branches broke as he pushed past them, while all the birds and the smaller animals of the wood fled from him in fear.

As he expected, the giant had no sooner come within reach of the tree where the cobbler was sitting than he stopped and sniffed the air around him.

'I smell human flesh,' he cried, and he looked up and saw the cobbler. 'So there you are! Come down at once, or I will break the tree under you.'

'Oh I will come down soon enough,' said the cobbler. 'But when I do you had better take care, for I should warn you that I am the strongest man in the world. Why, only last week I killed four hundred enemies with a single blow. I am far stronger than you, or any other giant in the whole tribe of giants.'

The giant stared at him disbelievingly. 'Prove it!' he said.

'Why of course,' said the cobbler. 'If you want me to prove it, I will.' He took out his balls of plaster-of-paris and cheese. 'Do you see these marble balls? Look —' and he tossed them into the air, and juggled them, and finally caught them one at a time and started to tear each one into shreds. 'That is what I do to marble.'

The giant was impressed in spite of himself. Strong as he was, he was not very brave or very intelligent, and he was easily hoodwinked. Giants, in fact, are never very intelligent; their brains are no bigger than an ordinary man's, and they work much more slowly.

So the giant stood there hesitating, watching the cobbler apparently breaking up marble balls with his bare hands. It was possible, he thought, that this man really was as strong as he claimed to be. It would be wiser not to take any chances.

'If you are as strong as all that,' he said finally, 'we might as well be friends. Come on down from that tree, come home to my castle with me, and we will have a good dinner.'

The cobbler climbed down out of the tree, and he and the giant walked on through the woods together until they came to the giant's castle. It was an enormous castle, dark and uncomfortable and very cold.

'The first thing we must do is to build a fire,' said the giant. 'But we have no wood. Do you mind going out to the forest and cutting up a few logs for me?'

. . . walked on through the woods together.

'Why waste time cutting wood?' the cobbler asked. 'If you don't mind my making a mess of your garden, and knocking a few smaller trees out of the way, I will drag in one of those big trees on the edge of the forest.'

The giant looked at the tree the cobbler was pointing to, which was enormous. If it were to fall in his garden, the garden would certainly be destroyed and it might damage the castle as well. 'Don't bother,' he said, 'we only need a little wood. I might as well cut it myself.'

He took his axe, quickly chopped up a few logs, and laid a fire in the castle grate. 'Now,' he said to the cobbler, 'we must have some water before we can start cooking dinner. 'You go down to the well there and fetch up a bucket of water.'

'A bucket?' the cobbler asked, with pretended surprise. 'Why bother with a bucket? Give me a strong rope, and I will drag the well itself up to the castle here.'

When he heard this the giant was even more frightened than before. Could it be true that this man could move an entire well? If so, the castle would be flooded and he himself might be drowned in the overflow. 'Never mind about moving the well,' he said, 'I will fetch the water we need.'

So it went on day after day. The cobbler took every opportunity of bragging about how strong he was and the giant, although he still had his doubts, was afraid ever to put him to the test. Even when the giant himself proposed a trial of strength, to see which of them could carry a heavy log on their shoulder for the longest time and the farthest distance, the cobbler insisted that the thick end of his log should be wrapped in a blanket – because, he said, he liked to turn somersaults while carrying heavy loads and he was afraid he might accidentally hurt the giant. The giant hesitated. Whereupon the cobbler went and took a blanket off the bed, and started wrapping it around the log. Then the poor, stupid giant believed him, lost his nerve, and refused to go on with the competition.

By this time the giant had had more than enough of

Very quietly he picked up a heavy iron bar which he had hidden

his guest, but he was so afraid of him that he did not know how to get rid of him. He decided that the only thing to do was to take him by surprise, when he was asleep, and kill him then. With this in mind, he insisted that the cobbler must sleep at least one night in the same room and in the same enormous bed in which he himself always slept.

The cobbler agreed to this readily enough. As soon as they were in bed, however, and had turned out all the lights, he put a large pumpkin on his pillow, just where his head would have been if he had really been sleeping there. He himself hid under the bed.

The giant waited until he thought the cobbler must be sound asleep and then, very quietly, he picked up a heavy iron bar which he had hidden on his own side of the bed. He brought this down over and over again, as

on his own side of the bed.

hard as he could, exactly where the head of the cobbler should have been, until he was quite sure that the man must be dead. The pumpkin was in fact smashed to a pulp. Thereupon the cobbler slid back into his side of the bed, pushing the pumpkin away, stretched himself, and yawned deeply.

When he heard this yawn the giant's heart sank down to his feet and he began to tremble with fear, so that the whole bed shook.

'What happened?' he cried. 'Are you all right?'

'I really don't know what happened,' said the cobbler sleepily. 'Something disturbed me just now. I think a flea must have bitten my ear – do you have fleas in your bed?'

By this time the giant was frightened out of his wits. He had no doubt now that this stranger was every bit as strong as he claimed to be. As he lay awake that night (and he lay awake the whole night through) he vowed to himself that he would take no more chances, nor propose any further trials of strength. On the contrary he would do whatever his unwelcome guest told him to do, hoping that in time he would go away of his own accord and live somewhere else.

On the following day however it was the cobbler himself who suggested a new competition. They would cook a huge cauldron full of macaroni, he said, and he would prove that he could swallow his half of it without chewing at all.

'I don't believe it,' said the giant suspiciously. 'Anyway, even if you swallow a whole bowl of macaroni without chewing it, you could never prove it. I cannot look into your stomach.'

'Oh yes you can,' the cobbler assured him. 'As soon

as we have had supper I will cut a narrow slit in my stomach and you will be able to see with your own eyes that I have not chewed even a single mouthful of the macaroni.'

He lit the fire, boiled the water, and cooked their supper. They both had as much macaroni as they could eat, with butter, cheese and tomato sauce. But the cobbler had tied a sack around his neck, hidden inside his coat, so that almost all the food he pretended to swallow actually went into the sack.

'Now look,' he said, when they had finished, and he slit the sack from top to bottom and let the macaroni spill out on the ground. Then he buttoned up his coat again. 'Why waste time chewing and digesting your food when it is as easy as that?'

'If you can do it, I can do it,' the giant retorted indignantly. Thereupon he slit his stomach open, and killed himself.

The cobbler cut off the giant's head and carried it back to the King. 'Here you are,' he said; 'Just let me know if you ever have any more trouble with other giants. And now, if you don't mind, I am ready to marry your daughter the princess.'

'She is yours,' said the King.

So they were married, and lived happily ever after. The cobbler never went in search of any further adventures. He did not need to. After all, everyone knew that he was the strongest man in the world, so he did not have to prove it. Everyone, even the few remaining giants who still lived in that part of the country, knew that he was a giant-killer; they quietly moved away to other districts, and were never heard of again.

ELEVEN

The Twelve Young Men

ONCE UPON A time two brothers, whose names were Cianne and Lise, lived next door to each other in the same city. But fortune had treated the brothers very differently. Cianne was a rich man, a merchant who had built up a trade in silk, spices and tea with the Orient; as the years passed his business prospered and he grew richer and richer, until there was almost nothing in the world he needed that he did not have. He built himself a large house, planted an orchard behind it, and lived there in great comfort. He travelled wherever and whenever he felt like it, bringing home many useful and valuable things with which to furnish his house.

Lise, on the contrary, was so poor that he had scarcely enough food to eat or enough clothing to keep him warm. However hard he worked it was all he could do to make a bare living. He lived in a little shack just beside his brother's big new house, and he thought himself lucky if he could find enough wood to build a fire in his grate on the very coldest winter nights.

You might have thought that in such a case the wealthy brother would have shared what he had with his less fortunate brother, but it was not so. Cianne not only kept what he had but he laughed at Lise for being so poor. He did occasionally send him a joint of meat, or a bundle of firewood, and he did invite him to come to dinner on Christmas and sometimes on other feast days, but he was always very condescending about it.

'If only you were as clever as I am,' he would say to

A little shack just beside his brother's big new house.

Lise, 'you too might have a fine house, and a fur-lined cloak, and servants to do your bidding.'

Finally Lise could stand it no longer. He put on his only pair of shoes, took his only coat, and set off to seek his fortune in some far country without even saying good-bye to Cianne. He wandered far and wide over the world, through many different lands, working at whatever came to his hand. He tended sheep in the high mountains, and he herded geese in the lowlands. He served as a deckhand on ships that crossed the western and the eastern oceans. He worked in the bazaars of the Middle East, and in the stables of Venetian princes. Wherever he went he earned enough to feed and to clothe himself, and that was all. He seemed no nearer to making his fortune than he had ever been.

One cold March evening he came to an inn, where he stopped to have some supper and to spend the night. It was a pleasant inn, with a blazing fire, and the landlord welcomed him and told him to make himself at home until supper was ready. A dozen young men were already sitting around the fire, warming themselves and chatting to each other, when Lise joined them. They all seemed to be about the same age, and they were apparently all old friends. Yet they were obviously men of very different character. Some were gay and laughed all the time, while others were cold and silent and scarcely said a word; some were dressed in bright-coloured silken garments, embroidered with gold or purple thread, while others wore dark brown or grey or even black clothes which were more suitable to the wintry weather.

The young men motioned to Lise to sit down near the fire, and he happened to find himself beside one of them who was rather melancholy in expression, and very sober in dress. This youth nevertheless smiled at him and made him welcome, striking up a conversation immediately:

'Well, countryman,' he said. 'What do you think of the weather? Is it not a dreadful time of year?'

'It is certainly cold,' said Lise. 'I must admit that I am very glad to be in out of the storm, warming myself here by the fire. But I do not think we should ever complain about the time of year. After all, we cannot expect summer in wintertime, nor flowers that will bloom in every season. Each month has its own place in the cycle of the passing year, its own task to perform, and we should be grateful to them all.'

'You are very tolerant,' said the youth; 'Surely, in spite of what you say, the month of March is the most unpleasant month of the whole year. Why must we have frost and rain, and hail and thunder all this time? We are longing for the warm, friendly touch of April and May. March is a miserable month, with its fogs and its storms and its everlasting cold.'

'On the contrary,' Lise argued. 'You should never speak ill of March. You are forgetting all the benefits that this month brings us, for without its rain and its fog the earth would never be ready for spring. It is the storms of March that prepare us for the flowers of April and May.'

The young man seemed unexpectedly pleased by these words. In fact all the youths laughed, agreeing with Lise, and one of them ordered the landlord to bring fresh wine so that they could drink to the month of March. After that they had supper, and a merry evening, retiring late to bed.

Next morning when Lise was setting off from the inn to continue his travels, his companion of the night before, the youth who had first spoken to him, presented him with a tiny box, covered with jewels.

'If you ever need anything,' he said, 'open this box and wish for it. You will see what happens.'

Lise thanked him, and went on his way. He had not gone very far, in fact he was scarcely out of sight of the inn, when he decided to find out whether the box was just a pretty toy or whether it really did have magical powers. Opening the box, he sighed, as though to himself.

'How nice it would be if I had a warm litter to carry me, instead of tramping through the snow.'

Almost before he had stopped speaking a litter had appeared beside him, with curtains, cushions, and two bearers waiting to carry him wherever he wanted to go. He stepped in, and off they went. A little later in the day he felt hungry and, opening the box, wished that he had something to eat. Immediately a table appeared before him in the road, with food for himself and food for his bearers as well.

As the day came to an end, and the cold March sun was setting, Lise looked around for an inn where he could spend the night, but there was not even a farmhouse to be seen. A narrow, sparkling stream ran along one side of the road he was following; otherwise he was alone in the midst of empty, rolling pasture land, apparently quite uninhabited. So he opened the box again.

'How nice it would be,' he sighed, 'if only I had somewhere to spend the night here by the river, instead of having to go in search of lodgings.'

The next thing he knew he was looking at a large, waterproof tent standing on the bank of the river. Two smaller tents nearby were apparently intended to provide shelter for his two bearers. The whole scene was illuminated by several flaming torches which were stuck in the ground outside the tent. Inside he found a scarlet couch, with a mattress of down and a pile of large, soft cushions. There was also a table set with gold and silver plates, knives and forks, with a delicious dinner waiting ready-cooked upon it.

Lise sat down contentedly to this meal. 'Somehow or other, I seem to have made my fortune,' he thought to himself; 'and if that is the case I need no longer wander from one end of the world to the other. I will go home and show Cianne how lucky I have been.'

Next morning he opened the little box and wished for a fine suit of clothes, so that he would not be ashamed to meet his brother again. He immediately found himself dressed in a black velvet gown, edged with fur, with a yellow travelling-cloak thrown over his shoulders and fur-lined boots on his feet. He stepped into his litter, told the bearers which road to follow, and very soon arrived at his native city.

Cianne stared at him in astonishment. 'Well, little brother,' he said, 'where have you been, that you have grown so rich?'

'I will tell you,' said Lise.

They sat down by the fire in Cianne's house and dined together. Lise told his brother the story of his travels, of the different lands he had visited, of the inn and the twelve young men he had found there, and finally of the magic box he had been given, which fulfilled his every wish. Cianne congratulated him on his good fortune. But late that night, when Lise was already fast asleep, Cianne lay awake thinking and thinking about the box and wishing that it belonged to him. Rich as he was, he could not resist the thought of a magic token which would bring him everything he wished for.

Thinking thus, it occurred to him that if he were to visit the same inn as his brother he too might receive an equally precious gift. The sooner the better. He got up at once, crept quietly out of the house without waking Lise, saddled his horse, and set off in the direction of the inn. He reached there the very next night, for it was no great distance away; although Lise had travelled the world over in search of his fortune his travels had brought him nearly home again, full circle, before he had stopped at that particular inn.

When Cianne went in he saw the same twelve young men whom his brother had described, some jolly, some sad, some quiet, sitting beside the fire and they promptly asked him to join them. He sat down in the same place near the fire that Lise had occupied, and the same rather melancholy youth put the same question to him.

'Well, countryman, what do you think of the weather? Is this not a dreadful time of year?'

'It certainly is!' Cianne agreed, shaking the snow from his coat. 'This month of March is the most unpleasant month in the whole year. March brings us nothing but storm and sorrow, fog and misery. It is well-named the enemy of the shepherd. As far as I am concerned we could do away with March altogether.'

The young man beside him said nothing, but he seemed more melancholy than ever, and less friendly. In fact if Cianne had not been so busy thinking about possible magic gifts he might have noticed how angry his neighbour had suddenly become. He might also have noticed that the other youths were all looking at their comrade sympathetically. For these twelve young men who always travelled together were of course the twelve months of the year, and it was the month of March who had first spoken to both Lise and Cianne.

Happily unaware of this, Cianne bade them all good night and went off to bed, confidently expecting that he would receive a present of some kind before he left the inn next morning. He was not disappointed. March came out to say good-bye to him as he was mounting his horse and presented him with a most beautiful whip, with thongs of fine leather and a pearl-studded handle. 'If you ever wish a surprise,' he told him, 'You need only say "Whip, give me a hundred." You will see what happens!'

Cianne was so excited that he wanted to try out the whip at once, and see what treasures his new magic toy would bring him. Fortunately, however, he decided he would wait until he got home and then he could show it off to Lise. As soon as he was inside his own house, he said to the whip – 'Whip, give me a hundred!' – and the next thing he knew the whip fell upon him and started beating him fiercely. It was so quick about this, dancing up and down over his back and his legs and his arms, that he had no hope of getting hold of it again and all he could do was to scream and cry out for his brother. Lise rushed in and when he saw what was happening he hastily took out his magic box, opened it, and begged the whip to stop. The whip immediately stopped beating Cianne and fell quietly to the ground.

'What on earth have you done?' Lise demanded of his brother.

Then Cianne confessed that he had gone to the inn in the hope of receiving a magic gift from the twelve young men. He told how he had talked to them, and how one of them had given him the beautiful whip he had assumed would make his fortune for him.

'It might have been a hundred rubies,' he said ruefully. 'Or a hundred bars of gold, or a hundred black slaves. How was I to know?'

'What a fool you are,' Lise retorted. 'You may be very clever in business, but you certainly have no common sense at all. I guessed, as you might have done, that the twelve young men who were so much alike, and yet so different, were probably the twelve months of the year and that in that case it was likely to be March who had spoken to me. But even if that thought never crossed your mind, why should you speak so unkindly about poor March? Every month plays the part it must, as best it can. It is quite true to say that the hard, wet weather of March prepares the way for all the beauty of spring.'

'You are right,' said Cianne, rubbing his legs tenderly, 'I had no reason to abuse poor March.'

'While you are about it, you might admit that you have had no reason to abuse me all these years past,' Lise pointed out. 'When you had money, did you ever think of giving me any? No, you only mocked me because I had none of my own. You were not even satisfied with your wealth; you wanted to have magic powers as well.'

Cianne threw himself on his knees and begged his brother's forgiveness. 'Do not worry,' said Lise, who was really very fond of his brother and knew that Cianne was foolish rather than wicked, thoughtless rather than cruel. 'We will forget the past. Hide away the whip where no one will ever find it again. My little box here will provide us both with everything we can possibly want for the rest of our lives, and there is no reason why we should not live at peace with each other.'

And so it came to pass.

TWELVE

The Parrot

In one of the cities of northern Italy, some years ago, lived a merchant. He was a rich man, and of noble blood. He was also a widower and he had only one child, a daughter, whom he guarded more carefully than any other of his treasures, for she was young and beautiful.

Now although her father very seldom allowed her to leave the house, it happened that both the Prince and the Viceroy of the province had passed by this girl's window and had seen her there and fallen in love with her. When they heard that the merchant was going away on a business trip, both Prince and Viceroy decided that they would try to meet the daughter and pay court to her while he was away. The Viceroy was the cleverer of the two men, and he felt quite sure that if a maiden had two suitors asking for her hand in marriage, and one was a Prince and one was a Viceroy, she would choose the Prince. So he made his plans accordingly.

In those days it was forbidden to practice witchcraft anywhere in the country. But the Viceroy knew perfectly well that some witches still carried on their magic arts in secret, and although in principle he might be opposed to witchcraft, in practice he did not hesitate to consult one of these when he needed help. He knew where to find the witch. He also knew exactly what he wanted her to do for him.

'If you will teach me how to turn myself into a parrot, and back again,' he said to the witch, 'I will pay you anything you ask.'

At first she denied that she could do such a thing. She

The transformation took a little time.

even denied being a witch, but when the Viceroy had explained who he was and promised that she would not get into any trouble, she agreed to do as he asked. The transformation took a little time. Nevertheless before the end of the day the Viceroy had become a parrot, a handsome bird with green feathers, a thick yellow beak and a most melodious voice.

The parrot flew off to a bird-market which was near

the merchant's house, and when the merchant rode by he sang and chattered away so cheerfully that the man bought him then and there and took him home to his daughter.

'Look what I have brought you!' he exclaimed. 'A talking bird. Now you will never again be lonely while I am away, for the parrot will talk and sing to you whenever you like.'

As soon as the merchant had set off on his travels, the parrot said to the girl – 'Shall I tell you a story?'

'Please do,' she said.

'What kind of a story would you like to hear? I know stories old and new. I can tell you about princes and princesses, or fairies or giants or magicians, or Heaven and Hell.'

'No,' she said. 'Tell me a story of merchants who travel overseas, like my father, and what they find there.'

'Very well,' said the Parrot, hopping from his perch down to the back of her chair, where she could hear him better, 'I will tell you the story of the Priceless Cats. But you must listen and pay attention, and you must promise me that if anyone comes to see you you will send them away and not interrupt the story.'

'I promise,' said the girl.

'This is the story about two merchants, both of whom lived in Venice,' he began. 'Now Venice, as you probably know, is a city of the sea. It stands on an island in the middle of a lagoon off the east coast of Italy, not so very far from here, and it has almost as many canals running through it as it has streets. So it is not surprising that the people of Venice are great seafarers and merchants. They trade with the Near East and the Far East and send their ships into every eastern country, to Persia, to India, and the Islands of Spice, to China and Japan.

'These two merchants that I speak of were called Don Giovanni and Don Cesare, and they were both very well off. Their ships carried cargoes of coral, and of lace, of glass and of bright-coloured beads, of toys and clocks and machinery out to Eastern ports, and returned with pepper and cinnamon and vanilla, for such spices are very valuable, and with silks and tapestries.

'Don Giovanni and Don Cesare were, however, men of very different character from each other. You must remember this if you are to understand the story.'

'I will remember,' said the girl.

'Don Giovanni was of a generous nature, always sharing whatever he had with anyone who needed it, always ready to help anyone who was in trouble. Don Cesare on the contrary prided himself on being a hard-headed businessman, always looking for a bargain, always wondering how he could make more money for himself.

'Now it happened that on one voyage Don Giovanni came to an island which he had visited before, where he expected to find a great quantity of spices. Instead he found that the island had fallen on evil days. The people were all extremely poor, and not one of them had enough to eat; everyone he met was complaining of hunger and poverty, but no one seemed to be able to explain to him *why* they were so poor when they had been so well off before.

'Finally one of the islanders took him to see their ruler. Thereupon Don Giovanni asked the King why this island, once so rich in spices, was now so poor.'

When the parrot had reached this point in the story

(and he took a long time telling it) a servant came in with a letter for the merchant's daughter. The letter was from the Prince, asking whether he could come to call on her, but the girl did not know that. And before she could open it the parrot, who was of course the Viceroy in disguise and knew perfectly well that the Prince was probably trying to get in touch with the merchant's daughter, interrupted her. 'Tell your maid to come back later,' he said, 'or we will never finish the story. I must tell you what misfortune had befallen the island of spices.'

So the girl sent the servant away, with the letter still unopened. She added firmly that she would not receive any letters at all until her father returned.

'Don Giovanni asked the King why his island was so poor,' the parrot repeated. 'And the King replied:

' "Why, it is because of the mice."

' "Mice?" said Don Giovanni.

' "Mice. There are thousands, hundreds of thousands, of them. They are eating everything on the island that can be eaten. They eat our corn, our spices, our bread – even our clothes. We catch a few in traps, but not many, and the others go on eating and eating and eating."

' "Surely, that is easily remedied," said Don Giovanni. "What you need are some cats."

' "I have never heard of a cat," said the astonished ruler. "What is it? Some kind of animal?"

'Don Giovanni laughed. "Yes indeed," he said. "A cat is a small, furry animal, whose greatest pleasure in life is catching mice."

' "How wonderful!" cried the King. "But these animals must be very rare?"

'This time Don Giovanni tried not to laugh. "There

are quite a few in my country," he said. "In fact, I have several on my own ship; I will gladly give you a couple if you like."

'He went back to the ship, and there he selected a handsome yellow male cat and a pretty little tabby female from among the many cats aboard, put them in a cage, and presented them to the King.

'Well, to make a long story short,' the parrot went on, although he was really making it as long as he could, 'the King was so overjoyed to have these wonderful cats (who set about chasing the mice just as soon as they were let out of the cage) that he rewarded Don Giovanni by giving him practically everything in the palace that had not been eaten by the mice – that is, ivory, sandalwood, precious stones, gold and silver.

'Don Giovanni sailed home well content. And soon after he returned to Venice he happened to meet Don Cesare one Sunday morning as they were both coming out of Saint Mark's Cathedral.

' "Well," said Don Cesare, "did you do well on your trip?"

' "Very well indeed," Don Giovanni told him. "I not only traded all the merchandise I was carrying at a good profit, but I visited one island – and he told him the name – where the King gave me so many presents, ivory and gold and scented wood, that I scarcely had room for it all."

' "How remarkable," said Don Cesare, thoughtfully. "Had you given him something particularly valuable, that he was so generous?"

' "Not really," replied Don Giovanni, who could guess what the other man was thinking. "All I gave him were two cats." '

At this point in the story a servant came in to tell the merchant's daughter that her aunt had come to call on her. Truth to tell, it was not her aunt, it was a messenger whom the Prince had sent pretending to be her aunt, but the girl did not know that. Neither did the parrot, who was of course the Viceroy. But he was taking no chances. 'Tell her to come back later,' he said, 'or you will never hear the end of the story.'

So the girl sent word that she could not receive visitors while her father was away, and that her aunt must come back another time. The parrot went on with his story:

'Now of course Don Cesare thought to himself that if Don Giovanni had received such rich presents in exchange for only two cats, all that he himself had to do was to visit the same island, carrying really valuable gifts for its ruler, and he would be even more richly rewarded. So he loaded his ship with glass vases, necklaces, Venetian lace, and chiming clocks, and set sail. It was a long, long voyage. But at last he came to the island, and was taken to see the King, and presented him with all the things he had brought.

'The King was of course delighted. He thought Don Cesare to be the most generous man he had ever met, not realizing that the merchant was only doing it in the hope of making a profit. In fact the King spent the whole day, and most of the night, wondering how he could possibly reward Don Cesare for his generosity.

'Next morning he called his councillors together. "This kind merchant, this Don Cesare," he told them, "has sailed all this long distance to bring us gifts. We can only repay him by giving him the most precious gift that it is in our power to give. And, as we know, the most precious thing in the world is a cat – or rather, two cats."

'Now by this time Don Giovanni's original two cats had had a good many kittens. There were enough cats on the island to keep the mice from doing much damage to the corn, or to the spices for which the island was famous. The councillors agreed that it would be possible

The parrot chuckled to himself.

to spare two of these valuable creatures. They chose two pretty kittens, they put golden collars around their necks, and placed them in a golden cage, and they presented the cage, very proudly, to Don Cesare.

'You can imagine,' and the parrot chuckled to himself, 'what Don Cesare thought when he saw the two cats. Just plain, ordinary cats. But he was a good fellow at heart, although greedy, and he could see that the joke was on him. Here on the island, a cat was undoubtedly the most valuable thing in the world. So he kept a straight face, he took the cats, and he said thank you, and sailed home again to Venice.

' "Well," said Don Giovanni, when the two men met again. "Did you have a good trip?"

' "Wonderful!" said Don Cesare. "I brought back the most valuable cargo I have ever carried in my ship." '

The merchant's daughter was delighted with this story. She insisted that the parrot tell her another story immediately, and another after that. She refused to do anything until her father returned except listen to the parrot telling his stories, day after day; she would not read a letter, nor see anyone, nor even leave her room. Which was of course exactly what the disguised Viceroy wanted.

As soon as it became known that the merchant had returned from abroad the parrot disappeared. The girl wept and wept, for she had loved her parrot and she did not see how she could ever live without the sound of his voice. But after her father actually reached home, bringing her presents from other countries far away, she thought less and less about the missing bird and listened to her father's stories of the places he had been and the cities he had seen with almost as much interest as she had listened to the parrot's tales.

Meanwhile the parrot flew off to the witch's cottage again. There, as soon as she had mixed together the right ingredients and spoken the right words, he reappeared in his original form as the handsome young Viceroy. Then he went home and immediately wrote a very polite, very formal note to the merchant asking for the hand of his daughter in marriage.

The merchant was pleased. He knew that the time had come for his daughter to marry, and he felt sure that the Viceroy would make her a good husband. So he agreed, and his daughter – although she had no idea that she had ever even seen the Viceroy – agreed, and the matter was settled. Preparations were made for the wedding feast to be held the very next day.

On the following day the Prince, hearing that the merchant had returned from his travels, also sent messengers to ask for the hand of his daughter in marriage. It was too late. Her wedding with the Viceroy was already being celebrated. She never knew, and her father never knew, that the unfortunate Prince had tried again and again to pay his court to the girl, and to tell her of his love for her, and had been outwitted by the Viceroy.

The poor Prince died of a broken heart, for he had loved her truly. But the Viceroy and his bride lived happily ever after, or at least for a very long time. And if the stories that he sometimes told her to while away the winter evenings seemed familiar, she only thought that he and her once-beloved parrot must have learned them from the same source.

THIRTEEN

Lionbruno

MANY OF THE Italians who live along the rugged coast of Italy earn their living as fishermen. They go out to sea almost every day in their little fishing-boats and are often gone all day, bringing home at night a good catch of fish, large tunny fish, small herrings and sardines, and sometimes squid and octopus as well.

Or at least they should bring home a good catch. At the time when our story opens the fishing along the shores of Italy had been poor, and getting worse, for several years. It was hard for any of the fishermen to make a living. The little boats still went out every day and cast their nets, dragging the sea for fish, but although they came home later and later they brought fewer and fewer fish.

One fisherman who lived in the south of Italy, always the poorest part of the country, was even worse off than most. He had been sailing and fishing all his life. Yet now he found it almost impossible to earn enough to support his wife and their children. Towards evening one day, when his boat was still empty, this fisherman cast his net for the last time and felt it catch on something heavy. He pulled it in very slowly and carefully, hoping that the fish he had caught would be big enough to feed his whole family that night – only to find that what he had caught was an empty, useless shell.

He flung the shell back into the sea. He turned his boat towards home. And as he did so he cursed the sea, and his boat and his fishing-net, and he cursed the Madonna and all the Saints to whom he had formerly prayed for a good catch.

He cursed the sea, and his boat and his fishing net.

Suddenly he was aware that someone had appeared in the midst of the sea beside his little boat. He could not see very well in the twilight, but he did think it strange that this person had no raft or boat and seemed to be supported by nothing more than the waves around him.

'Why are you so angry?' the apparition asked him.

'Why am I so angry! For three years I have scarcely

caught so much as one herring a day, and if things get much worse my wife will be begging in the village street. Now I pull in my net, as heavy as though it were filled with fish, and what do I find? A shell!'

'Well, well,' said the other. 'That certainly is bad luck. But I think I can help you. If you will just promise me that when the next son which is born to your wife is thirteen years old you will give him to me, I will see to it that meanwhile you and your family are prosperous. You will catch so many fish that you will have to be careful your boat does not sink under the weight of them, and you will sell them at such a good price that you can buy whatever you want. Your wife will never need to work again.'

When he heard this the fisherman knew that he was talking to the Devil. No one else would, or could, promise such things. And he knew that he should refuse whatever the Devil offered. But he was not only poor and desperate, he was a crafty man himself and he thought that he might be able to outwit the Devil. His wife was getting old, they had not had any children for several years now, and he did not think that they were likely to have another child. So he said to the Devil:

'That seems a fair offer. But if it is my next son you want, how can you be sure that I will have another son? What happens if I never do?'

'Don't worry about that,' said the Devil smoothly. 'I will honour my part of the bargain whatever happens. You will catch your fish, and make your fortune. If you never have another son – why, that is just my bad luck.'

Then the fisherman agreed, and swore a compact with the Devil. What he did not know, and the Devil did, was that his wife was in fact already expecting another child. She told him this news as soon as he reached home that night, and the fisherman cried out – 'May the Saints protect us. What have I done!'

His wife tried to comfort him, for she thought that he was only worrying about how they were going to feed another mouth. Fortunately she did not hear the ugly, mocking laugh in the distance which the fisherman could hear and which he knew meant that the Devil had tricked him into giving away his unborn son.

In the next few years the Devil was as good as his word. Wherever the fisherman cast his net, he drew it up heavy with fish. And the price of fish stayed high, so that he could always sell his catch at a profit. He and his wife and the children lived in great comfort. His wife was overjoyed by this change in their fortunes and she could never understand why her husband was so often melancholy, or why sometimes when she came upon him unexpectedly she found him weeping.

They named the new child Lionbruno. He grew up to be a handsome, intelligent and lively lad. And promptly on his thirteenth birthday, early in the morning, his father heard a harsh voice which he recognized as that of the Devil calling him: 'Mariner, Mariner, have you forgotten your promise?' He stepped outside the house and there was the Devil waiting for him.

'Send your youngest son down to the seashore today,' he said. 'Alone, and exactly at noon. I will meet him there.'

The fisherman did not dare disobey. But he had not the heart to tell either his wife or his son what he had done. He simply went off to fish as usual that morning, telling his wife to send Lionbruno down to the shore about midday to bring him some bread and some sausage for his lunch. Then he took his boat far out to sea, beyond sight of the land.

Lionbruno made his way down to the rocky beach early, well before noon, and when he realized that his father was nowhere to be seen he sat down on the sand to wait. He took out his knife, a bright, new pocket-knife which had been a birthday present, and whiled away the time by carving little wooden crosses out of the driftwood he found on the shore. As he finished each cross he stuck it upright in the sand beside him. So it was that when the Devil swept down, exactly at noon, to collect his prey, he found Lionbruno completely surrounded by a circle of crosses and still holding one cross in his hand.

Whatever else the Devil can do, whatever contract he may have, he can never touch anyone who holds a cross. Moreover the power of the crosses was such that as soon as the Devil, who had taken on the appearance of a harmless-looking old man, drew near them he was immediately revealed in his own dark and fearful form, with horns, flashing eyes, and a forked tail. Lionbruno gasped and shrank away from him.

The infuriated Devil thereupon ordered him to destroy the crosses at once. Lionbruno refused. But the Devil in his true form was very terrible, and finally the boy was frightened into breaking up the circle of crosses one by one. Still he would not give up the cross he was holding. The Devil coaxed and threatened and bargained with him, but the more he talked the more Lionbruno realized that his safety lay in the cross and the more firmly he refused to let go of it.

While the Devil was still shouting at him the Queen of the Fairies, a lovely young girl whose name was

Colina, suddenly appeared beside Lionbruno. 'Come with me,' she said. The Devil swore terribly, so that the sky darkened and thunder and lightning shot forth from the clouds, making people in nearby villages think that a sudden storm had hit the sea-coast, and he called on the angels of darkness to witness that Lionbruno was his. But Colina only laughed at him. It was now long past midday. She and the Devil both knew perfectly well that once he had failed to take possession of a soul at the appointed time, he no longer had any claim upon it.

Colina carried Lionbruno away with her to her own palace, far beyond Italy. There he grew up. And as he grew up he and the beautiful young Queen of the Fairies fell more and more in love with each other, until at last she promised to marry him and allow him to stay in Fairyland with her for ever.

The wedding day was set. Meanwhile, however, Lionbruno began to worry about his family. They had no idea what had become of him, or how happy he was, and they must believe that he had long since been carried away by the Devil. He asked Colina whether he could not possibly pay a short visit to earth, just to see his family, before they were married.

'Nothing could be easier,' she said. 'I will give you a magic ruby ring, which will enable you to travel wherever you like and do whatever you please. As long as you wear the ring, you have only to wish for something and it is yours.

'But if you love me,' she added, 'you must not be gone for more than twenty days. Otherwise you might lose me for ever.'

Lionbruno was delighted. He promised Colina that

he would return long before the twenty days had passed, kissed her good-bye and set off for his old home. He wore on his finger the magic ruby ring.

When he arrived home he found that his father and his mother and his older brothers and sisters were living in poverty, in what was little more than a hovel. It seemed that the Devil had been so furious over the loss of his intended victim that he had, perhaps understandably, taken away all the riches he had once bestowed on the fisherman and his family. They were as poor now as they had ever been in the worst days before Lionbruno was born.

Lionbruno did not make himself known at once. He asked for lodging, and although the fisherman was astonished that such a grand person as this visitor appeared to be should come to his little shack, he gave him the best room there was and did what he could to make the stranger comfortable. Imagine his astonishment when next morning Lionbruno, with the help of the ruby ring, turned himself into a youth of thirteen and revealed himself to his parents. He told them what had happened, and that now he was going back to marry the wonderful fairy Colina. Then he rubbed the ruby and asked for everything he could think of that would make his family happy: a fine house, servants, clothes, and a handsome new fishing-boat for his father. They feasted together for three days, eating, drinking, laughing, and enjoying themselves. Then Lionbruno bade them all farewell and set off on the journey back to Fairyland.

On his way there he came to a great city, a city at least as large as Naples, and spent the night at an inn. That very same night, as luck would have it, royal heralds rode through the city proclaiming that a tournament was to be held on the following day to see whether any knight was strong enough to pierce a great golden star and carry it away on his lance. Whoever won the tournament was to marry the King's daughter. Now Lionbruno was truly in love with the fairy Colina and he had no intention of marrying any King's daughter, but he felt sure that with the help of his ruby ring he could carry off the golden star and out of pure braggadocio he decided to go to the tournament.

He told the ruby what he wanted to do. Next day, therefore, when all the other knights and princes had taken their turn and had only succeeded in touching the star, Lionbruno rode up, pierced it and carried it away with him. He rode quickly back to the inn, where he hid the star and disguised himself. On the following day exactly the same thing happened. The King announced that since the knight who had carried away the golden star had disappeared, the tournament must be held again; again Lionbruno carried the star away with him, hiding himself at the inn.

On the third day the King proclaimed a third tournament. This time however he took the precaution of surrounding the palace with soldiers, so that before Lionbruno could make his escape again the guards captured him and brought him before the King. There he found the wedding feast already prepared and the King's daughter waiting for her bridegroom.

The Princess was undoubtedly beautiful. If Lionbruno had not already given his heart to the fairy Colina, he might have been glad to marry her. But as it was he looked at her, and smiled sadly, and said to the King:

'Your daughter, Sire, is very beautiful. But know

that I am already affianced to a maiden far more beautiful, a princess so fair that no one who has ever seen her could have eyes for another.'

The King and his nobles protested indignantly that Lionbruno was lying. No one on earth could be as lovely as their Princess. Furthermore they told Lionbruno that if he did not immediately produce his supposed fiancée and prove that she was in fact more beautiful than the King's daughter, then he must marry the Princess.

Poor Lionbruno did not know what to do. Finally he rubbed the ruby ring and wished for Colina to appear. The ruby however had no power over the Fairy Queen, for it was she herself who had bestowed all its magic upon the gem in the first place. And when Colina heard what had happened and that her lover was attempting to prove that she was more beautiful than some mere earthly princess she was so angry that she not only refused to go; she sent the lowest and homeliest of her serving maids in her place.

Unfortunately this girl, being also a fairy, was in fact more beautiful than the Princess. The courtiers and their King stared at her in astonishment.

'Your fiancée is certainly most beautiful,' they said.

'My fiancée?' Lionbruno laughed at them. 'Why, this is the lowest and the homeliest of her serving maids. This girl's beauty shines like a candle; my fiancée is the sun.'

When he heard this the King, thinking that his daughter had been insulted, was even angrier than before. He insisted that Lionbruno must either bring his true fiancée there at once or agree to marry the Princess. So Lionbruno rubbed the ring again, and again begged Colina to come. Again she refused, this time sending the second lowest and homeliest of her serving maids in her place, whereupon the same thing happened all over again.

The indignant King, having been tricked twice, now swore that this was Lionbruno's last chance. If his fiancée did not appear he must marry the Princess without further delay, or be put to death.

Under these circumstances Colina relented. At least she relented enough to appear suddenly in the middle of the throne room, where the startled courtiers were completely overcome by her unearthly radiance and murmured to each other that here indeed was the light of the sun. But she wasted no time listening to compliments. She went straight up to Lionbruno, her face dark with anger, and seized the ruby ring from his hand.

'You traitor!' she cried. 'Is this the way you repay my love, making me compete for your favours with some earthly princess who has charmed you away? Farewell then. You will never find me again – never; at least not until you have worn out seven pairs of iron shoes in search of me.' And she vanished before he could even speak.

The King now realized that Lionbruno had only won the tournament because he had been given magic powers and, far from offering him his daughter's hand in marriage, he indignantly ordered his servants to give the youth a sound thrashing and throw him out the back door of the palace. With the ruby gone, Lionbruno had also lost his horse, his escort and all his fine clothes. He found himself in the city square, alone, dressed like a beggar. He sighed, and wept, and then he wept again, knowing that he had brought all his misfortunes upon himself and had no one else to blame. Finally he made his way to the nearest blacksmith and asked him whether he could let him have seven pairs of iron shoes.

'That's easy enough,' said the smith; 'I can give you a dozen pairs if you like. But what makes you think you will live long enough to wear out seven iron shoes?'

'Never mind about that,' said Lionbruno. He took the seven pairs of shoes, put one pair on his feet, stowed three pairs in one side of his travelling knapsack and three pairs in the other side, and went sadly on his way. He walked and walked and walked. And no matter how far he walked, not even the first pair of iron shoes showed the least sign of wear.

After he had gone a very long way he found himself in a forest, where he fell in with some robbers. There were three robbers, and they were arguing fiercely about which one of them should have which of three precious objects they had just stolen: a pair of boots which would carry their owner faster than the wind; a purse which produced a hundred ducats every time it was opened; and a long cloak which rendered its wearer invisible. When they saw Lionbruno the robbers mistook him for a pilgrim, an obviously honest man, and agreed that he should divide the spoils for them.

'I will gladly settle the question for you,' said Lionbruno. 'But first I must be sure that these three things are what you say they are.'

He put on the boots, took a single step, and soared away like the wind. He came back, opened the purse, and there were a hundred ducats. Next he put on the cloak and started to button it up.

'Can you still see me?' he asked the robbers as he buttoned the next to the last button. 'We can see you,' they said.

Then he buttoned the last button. 'Can you still see me?' he asked. 'No indeed,' they said; 'You are quite invisible.'

'Well, if you cannot see me now, you never will,' said Lionbruno. He threw away the seven pairs of iron shoes, fastened on the boots that were swifter than the wind, took the purse full of ducats, and set off through the forest as fast as the boots would carry him.

He travelled a great distance, because he knew that wherever the palace of the fairy Colina might be it was very, very far away. And somewhere in the woods back of beyond he came upon a house, covered with ivy and almost hidden by dense shrubbery. He knocked on the door, but there was no answer. He knocked and knocked and knocked again, until finally it was opened by Borea, who is the mother of the four winds.

'Go away,' she said. 'This is no place for you. If my sons find you here when they come home they will eat you alive.'

'I am looking for the fairy Colina,' he told her. 'If your sons are the four winds, surely they will know where to find Colina.'

'That may be. But my sons like the taste of Christian flesh, and of human beings, and they are likely to have eaten you before they stop to talk to you. My son Sirocco has the most enormous appetite.' Then she looked at him kindly, and smiled, for Lionbruno was a handsome youth. 'Oh well,' she said, 'I will do the best I can for you. Hide in this chest here, and keep very quiet until tomorrow morning, and we will see what happens.'

Scarcely had the lid of the chest closed on Lionbruno when he heard the winds arriving. There was a moaning and a howling outside, trees shivered, branches cracked, and the ivy on the house had to cling tight to avoid being blown away. The door burst open and the winds poured in with a great clatter, the noisiest among them being the mischievous Sirocco.

'Oh but I am hungry,' he said, sniffing the air. 'What's this? I smell human flesh. Mama, dear Mama, are we to have human meat tonight?'

'Don't be silly,' said Borea. 'No human being would come to this wilderness. But there is a good supper waiting for you.' She went off to the kitchen and came back almost immediately with a huge dish of *polenta*, or porridge. They all sat down to supper, and soon Sirocco was so busy eating that he forgot the smell of human flesh.

Next morning the winds were feeling much less fierce and hungry than they had the night before. 'You made such a fuss about a human being last night,' said their mother Borea. 'What would you do now if there really *were* a human being here?'

'Last night I would certainly have eaten him,' said Sirocco. 'But this morning is different. The sun is shining, the whole world lies under our wings, and I at least have lost my appetite for men.'

'Do you promise that if one came here now you would not harm him?' his mother insisted.

Sirocco laughed. 'I was sure you had a human being hidden away somewhere last night,' he said. 'Never mind. I promise.'

She asked the other winds, and they also promised. So she opened the lid of the chest, and Lionbruno stepped out. The winds stared at him, puffed around him, and blew in his face, but they did him no harm. In fact they listened with interest when he told them of his plight, and his search, and of how he must find Colina's palace.

'Oh, I know where that is,' said Sirocco. 'I blow over it almost every day. Poor Colina. She is dying of love-sickness, thinking herself betrayed by her lover, and I make things worse by teasing her, rattling windows, shaking trees, and blowing under her doorstep.'

'Please, Sirocco, take me there,' begged Lionbruno. 'For I am the lover whom she thinks has betrayed her, and it is not so. I love her more than she could ever possibly love me.'

'I would take you if I could,' said the wind. 'But you could never stay on my back. I am wind and air and there is nothing to hold on to.'

'Don't worry about that. I can keep up with you,' Lionbruno assured him. The wind was not altogether convinced, but he agreed that if Lionbruno could follow him he would be willing to show him the way. They set off at dawn next day, and the only trouble was that Lionbruno's boots really were faster than the wind; he kept getting in front of Sirocco and every now and then he had to circle around and fall into place again behind his guide.

They reached the palace of the fairies at sunset. Sirocco insisted on blowing the windows of Colina's bedroom open with a great clatter and Lionbruno, who was now wearing the cloak of invisibility, quickly hid under the bed. Hearing so much noise, the servants came in to close the bedroom windows. Then Colina's maid came in with a cup of coffee and a cup of chocolate and tried to persuade her mistress to have something to eat.

'If you do not eat, you will die,' she said.

'Let me die,' said Colina. 'It is all the same to me.'

As soon as the maid had gone Lionbruno, who was tired and thirsty after his long flight, drank the coffee and the chocolate. When the girl came back again she was delighted to see the empty cups. 'At last you have broken your fast!' she cried; 'Now let me bring you something more nourishing.'

'You silly girl,' said Colina. 'I have not had even a sip of coffee, nor will I. Look, the cups are full.'

They both looked and both saw that the cups were empty. The maid ran away, terrified, to warn the other servants that a spirit of some kind must be hiding in their mistress' room. But Lionbruno thereupon came out from under the bed, took off the cloak of invisibility, and threw himself on his knees beside Colina.

'I have never loved anyone except you,' he told her. 'It was all a misunderstanding, all my fault, because I tried to show how clever and brave I was. I certainly would never have married that foolish princess who thought that she was beautiful. But you would not listen. You deserted me, disappearing before I could even explain.'

He told her the whole story, and she laughed, and they were happy again. It remained only to fix a new date for the wedding and arrange the wedding feast. They invited all the four winds, and their mother Borea, to come, but they warned Sirocco that he must not ask for human flesh. He did not seem to mind; there was plenty of *polenta*, *ravioli*, and noodles, and cake, and wine, and in the end Sirocco enjoyed himself even more than his brother winds.

FOURTEEN

The Griffon

UNTIL QUITE RECENTLY Italy, as we know, was divided into a number of separate kingdoms or princedoms, each with its own ruler. Now the King of one such kingdom, in northern Italy, was blind. He had lost his sight gradually, and he had never given up hope that his blindness was temporary and that he might one day be able to see again.

As the years went by he tried every possible treatment for his blindness, without success. Then at last a doctor in whom he had great confidence told him that there was one thing, and one thing only, which would ever restore his sight. If he could manage to obtain a feather from the wings of a Griffon, dip it in oil, and anoint his eyelids he would be cured.

This was by no means as easy as it sounds. The Griffon is a fabulous creature, half bird and half animal, who lives far away in the eastern mountains, in the direction of Persia, where the sun rises. He is sometimes called the Bird of the Sun, or Bird of Light, instead of the Griffon, and it is because he lives so close to the sun that his feathers have the magic property of restoring sight to the blind.

Many men, during many hundreds of years, have

come from different parts of the world in search of this remarkable bird. They have sought him for two reasons. First, because the touch of any one of his feathers can cure blindness. And secondly, because the claw of a Griffon, like the horn of a Unicorn, will immediately detect the presence of poison in any liquid, whatever it may be. A man who was lucky enough to find or steal a Griffon's claw would have it made into a drinking cup, and drink only from that cup; he knew that if an enemy ever put poison in his drink, the cup would at once darken, change colour, and become covered in sweat.

The Griffon, however, is an elusive bird, and fierce, and will not easily part with either a feather or a claw. Few of the men who hunted him had even caught a glimpse of him. Far fewer came within reach of him, or succeeded in carrying off a feather from his wing.

The blind King had three sons, who were now grown up. When he was told that nothing could possibly restore his sight except the feather of a Griffon he called his sons together and asked them all three to set forth in search of such a feather. At the same time he promised them that whoever first secured the Griffon's feather and brought it back to him should inherit the whole of his kingdom.

The three sons set off towards the sunrise. The two older Princes travelled together, being inclined to linger and enjoy themselves along the way. After all, they thought to themselves, it was most unlikely that they could ever find the magic bird, let alone pluck a feather from its wing. They had no liking for adventure, certainly not for such a hopeless quest as this. They would go as far as the first foothills of the Persian mountains, they decided, and then turn back and tell their father that it was impossible; sooner or later he would die and they would inherit the kingdom in any case. But the younger son walked and walked and walked towards the sunrise, as straight and as fast as his feet would carry him.

It was not long before the young Prince saw the eastern mountains rising high in front of him. They were still a long way off and they were the most forbidding mountains he had ever seen, steep, rocky and barren of all vegetation. His heart sank when he saw them, and his courage almost failed him when he thought of trying to penetrate into that wilderness. Nevertheless he walked on, and on, day after day.

As he drew near to the edge of the mountains he met an old man. They greeted each other warmly, as travellers do in such lonesome parts of the world, and talked together for a little while about the weather, and the time of year, and how cold it must be in the high mountains.

'Where are you going?' the old man asked him curiously. 'Not many people travel this way.'

'I am going to the mountains where the sun rises, to find the Griffon and pluck a feather from his wing, so that my father the King may regain his sight,' said the young Prince, and he sighed. 'I am afraid it will not be easy. They say that the Griffon is a wild, fierce bird.'

'It is true that he does not like to be disturbed,' said the old man. 'But he is also greedy. I can tell you how to steal a feather from his wing.'

'Tell me,' said the Prince.

'You must take this handful of corn' – and the man gave him a small measure of grain – 'And when you come to a certain place in the mountains, not far from here, which I will show you, you must sit down on the ground and put the corn in your hat. If you sit there long enough and still enough, like a statue, the Griffon will not realize that you are alive and he will eventually come flying down to eat the corn. Then you must seize him very quickly by the leg. You will not be able to hold him long, for he has strong wings and powerful claws, but you should have enough time to pull one feather out of his wing. As soon as you have done so throw yourself flat on your face on the ground and do not move a muscle until the Griffon is out of sight; otherwise he might well lift you up and carry you off with him into the mountains. I have seen him carry away an ox before now.'

These last words did not altogether reassure the young Prince. Nevertheless he thanked the man warmly, took the corn, and went on his way to the place in the mountains which his benefactor had pointed out to him. There he sat down on the ground, put the corn in his hat, and waited. He sat motionless, like a statue, scarcely daring to breathe, and waited.

It all came to pass as the old man had foretold. Suddenly there was a great rush of wings, the sky overhead was darkened, and he could feel that a huge bird was hovering above him, pecking at the grains of corn in his hat. He dared not look up. Instead he slowly, slowly raised one hand and grabbed the bird by its leg. Then he quickly put out his other hand and clutched a feather from its wing. The bird gave a great shriek, struck at the young Prince's hat with his claws, and soared away up into the air. The Prince was left holding the feather.

He threw himself flat on the ground and lay there

Suddenly there was a great rush of wings.

for what seemed a very long time. Then he rolled over on his back and looked around him. The sky was clear, without a cloud, the mountains were as barren and empty as ever; there was no sign of a bird, nor anything to show that one had ever been there. Nothing, that is, except the one precious feather he was holding in his hand.

Overjoyed by his success, the young Prince hid the feather in his left shoe to make sure that it was neither lost nor stolen, and set off for home. He had only gone a short distance when he met his two older brothers, who had just come within sight of the eastern mountains and were now thinking that it was time to turn back. The two brothers recognized him from far away, and the one said to the other:

'See how proudly our young brother walks, as though he had the whole world beneath his feet. He must have found the feather.'

'You are right,' said the second son; 'He has certainly found it.'

They walked a few paces in silence. Then the first son said to the other: 'Let us take the feather from him, and kill him, and leave his body here. We will tell our father the King that we two have secured the feather for him, and he will divide the kingdom between us.'

'You are right,' said his brother. 'That is what we will do.'

When the brothers had come up to each other, and greeted one another, the eldest asked the youngest whether he had found the Griffon's feather. Suspecting treachery, he said no, he had not found it. But the other two would not believe him. They fell on him and stripped him and searched his clothing, and at last they found the feather hidden in his left shoe. Then they killed him, buried his body there on the edge of the eastern mountains, and hurried home in triumph to give their father the feather and to claim the kingdom.

The old King dipped the Griffon's feather in oil and brushed it across his eyelids. Immediately he opened his eyes and he could see. He was so delighted that he embraced his two older sons, praised them for their courage, and divided the kingdom between them there and then. Somewhat later, he asked them about their younger brother.

'I thought you travelled to the mountains together?' he said. 'Why do you suppose he has not yet returned?'

'We travelled a little way together,' said the eldest Prince, 'but our young brother seemed to be in no hurry; he was enjoying himself along the way. So we finally left him behind, hurrying on towards the mountains of sunrise by ourselves.'

'And you did not meet him anywhere on your way home?'

'No,' the second Prince assured his father. 'We were anxious to bring you the feather as quickly as possible, so we took the shortest road. Our young brother probably turned aside somewhere to rest, or to amuse himself.'

As days and weeks and months went by and the young Prince did not return, the King reluctantly came to the conclusion that he must have been waylaid, or met with some accident. Perhaps if he had ever reached the land of the sun the Griffon had killed him, or carried him away to its lair in the farther mountains. The old King mourned his loss. But he was so delighted to have regained his sight that he could not be unhappy for long, and he thought less and less about the missing Prince.

Meanwhile in the eastern mountains a young shepherd who was in the habit of pasturing his sheep in the foothills thereabouts noticed that his sheepdog was always sniffing around and digging at one particular place. Wondering what the dog had found, and whether some treasure might not be buried there, the shepherd began to dig at that spot. He dug, and dug, until he had dug a deep hole, but all that he found was one small bone. It was a curious bone, shaped so exactly like a whistle that the shepherd, almost without thinking, put it to his lips. Immediately he heard a low whisper from the bone:

'Shepherd, keep me in your mouth, hold me tight, and do not let me go. For a feather of the Griffon, my brothers have played the traitor, have played the traitor' – and the whisper died away in a plaintive echo – 'The traitor, the traitor, the traitor....'

Astonished by this voice, although he had no idea what it meant, the shepherd kept the whistle and carried it with him wherever he went. Whenever he placed it in his mouth he heard the words repeated over and over again.

This same shepherd was in the habit of trading his sheep far and wide, in every part of the country. So it happened that in time he came to the city of the once-blind King, and passed by the royal palace on his way to the market. He had the whistle in his mouth at the time. The King, looking out of his window, saw the flock of sheep go by and heard a strange whistle, apparently coming from the lips of the shepherd, as they passed;

it was a sound unlike any he had ever heard, more like the moaning of the wind than a shepherd's tune. Curious, he ordered his servants to bring the man up to the gate of the palace, where he could speak to him.

'What are these words you keep whispering to yourself as you drive your sheep to market?' he asked.

'I do not whisper them, Your Majesty,' the shepherd assured him. 'It is this bone, like a whistle, that I found in the mountains.' And he told him the story of his sheep-dog, and how he himself had dug into the earth in search of treasure and unearthed the bone instead.

The King took the bone, looked at it with interest, and placed it in his own mouth. 'Papa!' he heard, 'Papa! Keep me in your mouth, hold me tight, and do not let me go. For a feather of the Griffon, my brothers have played the traitor, have played the traitor, the traitor. . . .'

'What on earth does this mean?' cried the King, horrified. 'Is it possible that my older sons betrayed their brother for the sake of the feather they brought me, and the kingdom I promised them?'

He questioned the shepherd more closely about when and where he had found the bone. 'In the foothills of the eastern mountains, the mountains of the sun,' the man replied. 'Not far from the land of the Griffon.'

The King now called his oldest son, who had already succeeded to half of the kingdom. Without a word of explanation he asked him to put the whistle to his lips for a moment. No sooner had it touched his lips than the Prince, the King and the shepherd could all hear the voice, which seemed louder now, crying out: 'Brother! Brother! Keep me in your mouth, hold me tight, and do not let me go. For a feather of the Griffon, you have played the traitor, have played the traitor. . . .'

'What is this nonsense?' cried the Prince. But he had turned white as a ghost, and he pulled the whistle out of his mouth and threw it violently away into some bushes nearby. The shepherd quickly went and picked it up again, handing it back to the King.

Thereupon the King called his second son, who had succeeded to the other half of the kingdom. He commanded him to put the whistle to his lips. Exactly the same thing happened all over again. The two Princes stared at each other in horror as they realized that somehow the truth was known. And the King took the whistle in his hands again, and wept, for now he knew what fate had befallen his youngest son. Indeed the two conspirators soon confessed the whole story; they could scarcely deny their guilt when the evidence had come from their own lips.

The King condemned his two sons to death, and they were executed. But, alas, he had no means of restoring the younger boy to life. All he could do was to carry the whistle with him as long as he lived, listening to its plaintive echo and lamenting the death of the brave Prince who had actually succeeded in obtaining the Griffon's feather for him and thus restoring his sight. He no longer took any great pleasure in the fact that he could see. He would gladly have been blind again, he sometimes thought to himself, if he could have had his youngest son beside him once again.

That is the end of the story, according to some storytellers. Others say that although he could not bring his own son back to life, the old King did not die without an heir to the throne. He adopted the shepherd who had brought him the whistling bone as his son and heir. And this youth, so they say, came to resemble the dead Prince more and more as the years went by; he finally inherited the whole of the kingdom and ruled wisely and well for a long, long time.

FIFTEEN

Padre Ulivo and His Guests

IN A LITTLE village, scarcely larger than a hamlet, on the road from Ostia to Rome there once lived a man who was known to everyone in the neighbourhood as Padre Ulivo, or Father Ulivo. Padre Ulivo was a poor man, but he was generous and always ready to share what he had with those who were poorer than himself. Pilgrims on the way to Rome, peasants who were out of work, beggars, all stopped at his little house when they were in need. They knew that he would give them anything he could possibly spare.

One winter day, about noon, Padre Ulivo heard a knock on his door. He opened it, and his heart sank. There at the door were no less than a dozen pilgrims, all of whom looked hungry and thirsty and cold. And Padre Ulivo knew very well that he had only half a loaf of bread in his cupboard, half a bottle of wine in his cellar, and no firewood at all to put on the embers of his dying fire.

'Well,' he thought to himself. 'A dying fire is better than none; a crumb and a sip of wine are better than an empty stomach.'

Aloud he said, 'Come in, come in!', welcoming his unexpected guests as warmly as he could. He led them to the fire, or what was left of the fire, and found enough chairs and benches for all twelve of them to sit down.

'I am sorry I have so little to offer you,' he told them. 'I was not expecting many pilgrims to come this way at this time of year. There is only one loaf – no, half a loaf – of bread in the house.'

'Do not worry,' said the man who seemed to be in charge of the party of pilgrims, 'I am sure that half a loaf will do us very well.'

Padre Ulivo went into his kitchen and opened the cupboard where he kept his bread. To his astonishment he found there a baker's dozen, which is thirteen, small loaves of fresh-baked bread. What was even more surprising was that on the shelf above, which he knew perfectly well had been bare an hour before, was a whole Gorgonzola cheese and more than a pound of fresh butter.

He carried all this back to the room where his guests were warming themselves by the fire. 'By some miracle —' he started to say, and then he stopped dead, staring at the fire. Half a dozen good pine logs were crackling merrily away in the grate, with flames high up the chimney, where before there had been only a few charred and broken sticks. Several other logs were stacked beside the fireplace.

By this time Padre Ulivo realized that a miracle really was happening. He decided that it would be better not to be surprised by anything, or at least not to show his surprise. So he simply spread the table for his visitors and invited them to come and eat.

'Have you any wine in your cellar?' asked the leader of the pilgrims.

'Half a bot —' began Padre Ulivo, and then he stopped himself. 'I will go and see,' he said.

He was not really surprised when he climbed down into the cellar to find a dozen bottles of good red wine on shelves that he had seen empty that very morning.

So it was that Padre Ulivo and his guests had a good meal, beside a warm fire. When they had finished the party took their leave, saying that they hoped to reach Rome that night, and each one shook Padre Ulivo by the hand and thanked him for his hospitality. When the last of the pilgrims, who was also the youngest, came to say good-bye, he said to Padre Ulivo:

'You should have asked our leader for a boon. He would have granted you anything in the world, or for that matter out of the world, that you asked him for.'

'How can he do that?' asked Padre Ulivo.

'Do you not, then, know who we are?'

'I do not,' said Padre Ulivo. 'Except that you are clearly no ordinary band of pilgrims.'

'We are the disciples of Christ,' said the young man. 'And He who leads us is our Lord himself.'

When he heard this Padre Ulivo ran after the Leader of the supposed pilgrims, fell on his knees and kissed the hem of His robe.

'Will you grant me a boon?' he asked.

'Gladly,' said the Lord; 'What is it you want?'

'I would like it to be so that anyone who sits down in the chair beside my fireplace is unable to rise again unless I wish him to do so.'

'Well, if that is what you want, so be it,' said the Lord.

He went on his way. Then the youngest disciple, who

had been listening, said to Padre Ulivo: 'That is a foolish wish. Ask for something else.'

'Do you really think I could ask another boon?'

'I am sure you could.'

So Padre Ulivo ran after the Lord again, and asked for a second boon.

'Gladly,' said the Lord. 'What is it you want?'

'I should like it to be so that if anyone climbs the cherry-tree in my garden he cannot come down again until I wish him to do so.'

'Well, if that is what you want, so be it,' said the Lord.

The youngest disciple, having also listened to this conversation, sighed. 'What did you want to ask that for?' he said. 'It will do you no good to have someone stuck in your cherry-tree. Ask for something else.'

'You mean I could ask yet another boon?' said Padre Ulivo.

'I think so. But that will be the last. No man ever receives more than three boons.'

So Padre Ulivo ran after the Lord again, and asked for a third boon.

'Very well,' said the Lord. 'But this is the last one. What do you want?'

'I want it to be so that if I play at cards, I always win.'

'Well, if that is what you want, so be it,' said the Lord.

Then He and His disciples went on their way, shaking their heads sadly over the foolishness of mankind. 'He could have asked for the salvation of his soul,' said the youngest disciple, 'or he could at least have asked for long life, or happiness, or wealth here on earth.'

'I know,' said the Lord. 'But you could not tell him that. He had to choose for himself. Let us hope that at least his three foolish wishes will do him no harm.'

In fact for a long time Padre Ulivo's three boons made no difference to his life at all. He never played cards. And he had no reason to keep anyone sitting in his chair, or up the cherry-tree.

It was one day in February, many years later, that a thin, dark man knocked on the door and said to Padre Ulivo, 'Come with me.'

'I know you,' said Padre Ulivo. 'You are Death.'

'Yes.'

'Well, I suppose it is no use arguing with Death,' said Padre Ulivo. 'If you want me, I must come. Just give me a few minutes to get ready. Here – sit down in the chair by the fire.'

Death sat down. A few minutes later Padre Ulivo said that he was ready to go, and Death started to get up, only to find that he could not.

'What have you done?' he demanded angrily, trying to push himself out of the chair; 'What sort of a trick is this?'

'An enchanted chair,' said Padre Ulivo, as though it were the most natural thing in the world. 'You cannot get up until I want you to.'

'How long do you propose to keep me here, then? I cannot waste time like this; I have work to do.'

'Only until you promise to go away and not come back again for another three hundred years.'

Death promised. He could not really do otherwise, unless he was willing to go on sitting beside the fire for all eternity.

Three hundred years went by. As far as Padre Ulivo

was concerned, they went much too quickly. He was still enjoying life when Death returned at the end of the three centuries, and he wanted to go on enjoying it. 'Just make yourself comfortable,' he said to Death, 'while I get ready.'

'You can have exactly five minutes to get ready,' Death told him sternly. 'And no more of your tricks, mind. I am not going to sit down anywhere while I am waiting.'

'I don't blame you,' said Padre Ulivo sympathetically. 'Why not go out in the garden and wait for me there?'

So Death unsuspectingly walked out into the garden, which was really not much of a garden, being small and neglected. It did however have a few fruit trees, including one cherry-tree whose branches were heavy just then with beautiful ripe black cherries.

'Help yourself to the cherries,' Padre Ulivo called out of the window. 'I won't be needing them, I will be dead so soon.'

Death picked a few of the cherries and found that they were as good as they looked, or even better. But of course, as always happens, the biggest and best fruit was just beyond his reach. So it was that Death, quite without thinking, climbed a little way up the cherry tree. Then he climbed further and further, picking only the very best of the cherries.

'I am ready,' said Padre Ulivo from the bottom of the tree a few minutes later. 'Shall we go?'

Death started to climb down. But he could not move. Or, rather, he could go on climbing up but the minute he tried to take a step down he was stuck.

'You wretch!' he cried. 'You have tricked me again.'

'I am afraid I have,' chuckled Padre Ulivo. 'How about another three hundred years?'

Once again, Death promised. He really had no choice.

Padre Ulivo enjoyed his next three centuries almost as much as the last three. But he knew he could not live

Death picked a few of the cherries.

for ever. The next time Death came he was ready and waiting for him – which was just as well, because Death stood outside the gate, looking neither to the right nor the left, and shouted at him. 'Come at once!' he cried. 'And no more tricks this time. I am waiting right here until you come.'

Padre Ulivo took a last look at the little house where

he had lived for six hundred and sixty-one years, and sighed, and then he went along with Death.

'About time too,' said the latter. 'But you have nothing to worry about. You just follow that road there up to Heaven; I suppose, in spite of your tricks, that you will be allowed into Heaven.'

Padre Ulivo thereupon set off along the winding road that led to Heaven. He had only gone a very short distance when he came to the outer gate of Hell, and saw the Devil sitting there, and heard the voices of a great many of the souls in Hell calling out for help. He stopped.

'What do you want?' the Devil demanded suspiciously.

'I am on my way to Heaven,' Padre Ulivo told him. 'And I am afraid that once I am inside Heaven I will never get a game of cards again. I was thinking how nice it would be to have one last game.'

'Why not?' said the Devil, thinking he saw a way to get Padre Ulivo into Hell instead of Heaven. 'I will play with you.'

He brought out the cards and Padre Ulivo sat down beside him, there at the entrance to Hell. 'What do you want to play for?' the Devil asked him.

'My soul,' said Padre Ulivo promptly; 'My soul against a dozen of the other souls you already have here in Hell.'

The Devil could hardly believe his ears. He knew every card trick there was; he had never yet lost a game to anyone. And here was this foolish man offering to gamble his own soul away! 'That suits me,' he said, dealing the cards.

Of course Padre Ulivo won. The Devil had to release

a dozen souls from Hell and hand them over to his opponent. Moreover he was so sure that there had been a mistake, and that he could not possibly lose another game, that he insisted on playing with Padre Ulivo again, and again, and always for the same stake.

They played and played. Each time Padre Ulivo won another dozen souls. Finally, when Hell was almost empty, the Devil realized that he had been tricked and that he could never win. He threw the cards angrily down on the ground, slammed shut the gates of Hell, and disappeared. Padre Ulivo shrugged his shoulders and started off again on his way towards Heaven.

He was however now followed by several hundred other souls, who, having thus unexpectedly escaped from Hell, had nowhere else to go. When this crowd arrived at the gates of Heaven Saint Peter looked at them scornfully.

'What are you all doing here?' he demanded. 'You people have no right to enter Heaven. Go back where you came from at once.' Then he turned to Padre Ulivo. 'You can come in,' he said. 'Even though you have been behaving rather strangely recently, I think you have enough credit in Heaven to be allowed to enter.'

'Don't be silly,' said Padre Ulivo. 'How can I leave these hundreds of souls outside, while I come in? They belong to me. They will have to come into Heaven with me.'

'That is quite out of the question,' Saint Peter retorted.

'Well then, before we go, will you give the Lord a message for me?' asked Padre Ulivo.

'If you like.'

'Just tell the Lord that when he came to the gate of

my house, I did not ask Him who his friends were, or say that they were too many to come in. I opened the door to them all. Ask the Lord, please, whether He wants to have it said that a poor human being is more hospitable than He himself?'

The answer that came back was what Padre Ulivo had known it must be. He and his friends, whoever they were and however many they might be, were welcome in Heaven. And so Padre Ulivo, as a result of his three foolish wishes, not only saved his own soul but a great many others as well.

SIXTEEN

Oraggio and Bianchinetta

IN THE NORTH-EASTERN corner of Italy, not far from the sea, lived a noble lady whose husband had died only a few years after they were married and who was left alone to take care of her son, Oraggio, and her daughter, Bianchinetta. Things went badly with her. One misfortune after another befell the family, until by the time the children were grown up they had been reduced from wealth to poverty. There was no money left to provide a dowry for Bianchinetta and her mother often wondered, beautiful though the girl was, how they would ever find a husband worthy of her

Oraggio, who was the elder of the two children, knew well what his mother was thinking. So he said to her one day, 'Mother, I must go into some far country and make my fortune there. If all goes well I will either return to you, bringing enough money to provide a dowry for Bianchinetta, or I will send for my sister to come and join me.'

He travelled across the sea and came to another country, and there he offered his services to the Prince, to use as he saw fit. The Prince first agreed to employ him as a *valet de chambre*, a very humble occupation, but when he discovered that Oraggio was of noble birth and well educated he promoted him to be Keeper of the Royal Pictures. Thereafter Oraggio spent all his time in the picture gallery of the palace, where the Prince had a fine collection of portraits, landscapes and sculpture. He enjoyed this work, for he was something of an artist himself and particularly fond of portraits. But he was still a long way from making his fortune.

There was one portrait in the collection that he admired above all the others, partly because it was so well painted but even more because it seemed to him that it was exactly like his sister Bianchinetta. The girl in the picture had the same milky-white skin, the same enormous black eyes, the same blood-red lips. The more he looked at her the more the resemblance grew. He would often stand in front of the picture for hours at a time, remembering his sister, talking to her reflection in the portrait, and wishing that he could see her again.

Finally the Prince noticed how much time Oraggio spent staring at this particular painting, almost as though he expected it to come to life. 'Tell me,' he said to the youth one day, 'why do you spend so much time admiring this picture? There are many other excellent portraits in the collection.'

'It is because this maiden here, whoever she may be, is so like my own sister that they might well have been twins.'

'You must be mistaken,' said the Prince. 'No girl alive, no girl of flesh and blood, could be as beautiful as the unknown maiden you see here.'

Oraggio started to speak, but the Prince stopped him. 'Let me tell you why I am so sure of this,' he went on, with a melancholy smile. 'It is because I myself fell in love with this portrait when I first saw it, years ago. Thereafter I travelled far and wide in search of some princess who might resemble this imaginary beauty. I sent messengers east of the sun and west of the moon, seeking any maiden who might be as fair as this. But it was all in vain. It is for that reason that I remain, and will remain, unmarried.'

'Nevertheless, Your Highness,' Oraggio insisted, 'I assure you that my sister Bianchinetta, so named for the whiteness of her skin, is so like this painting that you could not tell the one from the other.'

'Bring your sister here,' the Prince told him. 'If what you say is true she shall be my wife.'

Oraggio immediately wrote to his sister and asked her to join him as quickly as she could, on the same ship which carried his letter. And when he knew that it was time for the ship to be nearing port on the return journey he went down to the seashore every day to watch for it, praying that Bianchinetta would arrive safely and that she would still be as beautiful as he remembered her. 'Oh mariners of the high sea,' he prayed, 'guard my sister Bianchinetta, so that the sun shall not brown her, nor the salt wind darken her skin.'

Unfortunately there happened to be another young girl, of about the same age, travelling on the same ship as Bianchinetta. When this girl discovered that Bianchinetta was on her way to marry the Prince of the far country she was so jealous that she was determined to prevent the marriage at all costs. Worse than that; she decided that she would take the place of Bianchinetta and marry the Prince herself.

The ship was already within sight of land when this

girl, whose face was as dark and ugly as her disposition, crept quietly up behind Bianchinetta where she was standing on the deck, gave her a quick shove and pushed her overboard into the sea. No one else noticed what had happened. The girl then went down to Bianchinetta's cabin and dressed herself in the best clothes she could find there, with a veil that would shade her face. As soon as the ship touched shore and the gangplank was laid down she hurried off the ship and threw herself into Oraggio's arms.

'Oh my dear brother!' she cried.

Oraggio, naturally enough, did not recognize her. 'What has happened?' he cried. 'Why is your face so dark and so different?'

'It is the sun,' she said. 'The sun and the salt water and the wind have darkened my skin a little. Now that I am safely ashore I will soon recover that fair skin you remember so well.' Then she looked impatiently around her, and saw the towers of the royal castle, which stood on a hill beyond the city. 'Take me to the Prince at once,' she said; 'I am eager to meet my bridegroom to be.'

Reluctantly, Oraggio did so. Although he felt sure that this was not his sister, there was nothing he could do about it. She had come on the ship on which he knew Bianchinetta was travelling, and she called him brother. He even recognized the dress she was wearing. Perhaps it was true that the sun and the salt wind could make such a change; perhaps she lay under a spell and would recover.

When the Prince saw the supposed Bianchinetta he flew into a great rage. He would listen to no explanations, no talk of spells or salt winds or sun. He took the girl and made her stand beside the portrait, and he said to Oraggio – 'You must be mad. Look – even if the skin were fair, look at those tiny eyes, that thin mouth, that hideously long nose! I will certainly not marry your sister.'

He ordered the girl to be thrown into a dungeon, dark enough to match her complexion. Then he turned to Oraggio again. 'I never really believed that your sister or anyone else could be as beautiful as the girl in this painting,' he said, 'but I did not think that you would deliberately deceive me; I thought there might at least be some resemblance. If that is all you know about beauty, you are certainly not fit to look after my paintings. You can go out and take care of the geese instead, and listen to their cackling.'

So Oraggio was set to watch the royal geese. All day and every day he herded them from the palace down to the seashore, and back again, sighing as he did so for his lost sister Bianchinetta.

Bianchinetta meanwhile had not been drowned when she fell ino the sea. She sank far down, down and down, until she was almost fainting from lack of air and from the weight of the green waters above. Then suddenly she found herself lifted up and carried away on the back of a large fish, something like a dolphin. And all at once she was able to breathe again; thereafter she could breathe with equal ease in the air or in the water, feeling perfectly comfortable in either element.

The fish swam only a little way before they came to a palace under the sea, with coral gates and walls built from mother-of-pearl shells. This was the home of one of the Dragon Kings, the ruler of a vast underwater kingdom and monarch of all the fish who lived for many miles around. The Dragon King was delighted when Bianchinetta was brought to him. He had never before seen anyone so lovely, so fair-skinned, and he immediately decided that he would keep her with him there in his underwater kingdom for ever. She would be better off there than she had ever been on the earth's surface, he told her; she would live like a queen, with fish of every kind to wait upon her, with pearls and coral and all the jewels of the sea for her very own.

The Dragon King was as good as his word. Bianchinetta wanted for nothing. She had so many servants that there was really nothing for them all to do; big fish and small fish, quick-swimming fish that darted here and there to bring her anything she needed, quiet, intelligent fish who showed her all the curious and beautiful things to be seen at the bottom of the sea and taught her to recognize the different flowers growing there, the shells and the sea-grasses. The underground palace itself, built on white sand, with coral trees, tall, flowering seaweed, and a curious green light that filtered down through the waves, was very beautiful. Yet poor Bianchinetta never ceased to pine for the world above, longing for the feel of dry land under her feet, for the sky above her, and the hills of Italy.

Every day she begged the Dragon King to let her go. Every day he refused. But at last, seeing how unhappy she was, he relented a little.

'Very well,' he said. 'You may go up to the shore where the sea and the earth meet. You may go there every day if you like, breathing the thin air of dry land. But I will not let you leave me – no, not so long as you live.'

He fastened a long, long chain, light in weight but so strong that no sword could cut through it, around her ankle. She could swim and she could walk, scarcely feeling the chain, but she could not escape; she was actually chained to the palace and could never go further than the seashore.

Bianchinetta nevertheless went up to the shore as often as she could, walking along the wet sand, watching the seagulls, seeing the blue sky overhead and looking out across the world she had lost. There one day she met Oraggio, herding his geese down to the water's edge. At first they were both so astonished they scarcely knew what to say, and then they both started to talk at the same time, weeping and laughing together. Oraggio told her all that had happened, how another girl had come in her place, an ugly creature, and how the Prince was so angry at what he thought was a trick of Oraggio's that he had turned him out of the palace and set him to looking after the geese. Bianchinetta told him how the girl had pushed her overboard and how she had been captured by the Dragon King; how she lived under the sea and could not get back to earth again.

After that they used to meet on the beach every single day. Bianchinetta would sing to her brother, whiling away the time by adorning his geese with bright coloured tassels and ribbons which she plucked from her own dresses, feeding them titbits which she brought up from the palace under the sea.

The geese thoroughly enjoyed all this attention. When they were driven back into the palace courtyard each night after the sun had set they would chatter and cackle away to themselves about their good fortune.

'Crò! Crò!' they said,
'From the sea we come;
We feed on gold and pearls.
Oraggio's sister is fair,
She is fair as the sun,
She would suit our master well.'

They were both so astonished they scarcely knew what to say.

One day the Prince heard them cackling away. He listened in surprise, and he listened a second and a third time as they repeated their little ditty. Then he summoned Oraggio and said: 'What is the meaning of this?'

Oraggio told him the whole story. How an imposter had pushed his unfortunate sister overboard and had

taken her place; how Bianchinetta had been carried away to a kingdom under the sea and was still chained to the Dragon King's palace there, so that they could only meet at the edge of the seashore.

'If what you say is true,' said the Prince, 'ask your sister what must be done to set her free. But,' he added, 'if I do rescue her, and she is not as beautiful as you have said, it will go ill with you.'

'Have no fear,' said Oraggio; 'If you see my sister, you will not be disappointed.'

Next day he hurried down to the beach as soon as it was light to meet Bianchinetta and tell her that the Prince was determined to rescue her and bring her back to earth.

'Alas,' she said, 'it is impossible.'

'Nothing is impossible,' Oraggio told her bravely.

'The Dragon King himself told me that is was impossible,' she said. 'This chain, although so light, can never be broken except by a sword that cuts more keenly than a hundred other swords. Even if the chain is cut, I could never get away unless I had a horse that runs faster than the wind; the Dragon King himself is as fast as the wind and he would soon overtake me.'

'Well,' said Oraggio, 'it is lucky that the Dragon boasts so much about the strength of his chain, and his own speed. At least we know what it is we need.'

He went back and told the Prince exactly what his sister had said. 'If that is how it is,' said the Prince, 'I must find a sword that cuts like a hundred other swords, and a horse faster than the wind.'

He set off at once in search of these treasures. He was gone for a year and a day, travelling to countries he knew and countries he did not know, towards sunrise and sunset, north and south. He had many adventures on the way, which do not concern us here, but he was young, and determined, and a Prince, and he had friends to help him. After a year and a day he returned to his own palace, bringing back with him both the sword and the horse.

Then Oraggio and the Prince went down to meet Bianchinetta at the water's edge. The Prince saw at once that she was every bit as beautiful as the portrait he had loved for such a long time, perhaps even more beautiful. Her skin was milky-white, completely unharmed by the touch of salt water, her eyes were large and dark, her lips were as red as blood on the snow. As soon as they had greeted each other she explained to them that the chain around her ankle could only be broken in the underwater palace itself, where it was made fast. The Prince and Oraggio therefore followed her down deep below the surface of the water, where, to their own surprise, they found that they too were able to breathe under water without any difficulty.

The Prince cut through the base of the chain with a single stroke of his sword. He made so much noise that the palace guards and the Dragon King himself were aroused, and they all hurried to the spot to try to recapture their lovely prisoner. By that time however Bianchinetta was already mounted on the horse that was swifter than the wind; the Dragon King had no hope of overtaking her, for within a very few seconds she had reached the shore and was safe on land again.

The Prince and Bianchinetta were married on the following day. The jealous, ugly imposter who had tried to murder Bianchinetta and take her place was condemned to be burnt in the public square of the city. As for Oraggio, he went back to his work as the Keeper of the Royal Pictures, where he was happy ever after.

SEVENTEEN

Giufà

GIUFÀ WAS THE son of an old country woman who lived on the east coast of the island of Sicily. He was not very bright. Moreover, he believed everything that anyone ever told him, even if it was the most obvious nonsense. He was the despair of his mother, because although he did whatever she asked him to do, and many other things beside, he almost always got it wrong and ended up with things a good deal worse than they had been before.

Giufà tried hard to be helpful. So one day, knowing that his mother had some pork she wanted to sell in the village market, he said to her:

'Let me take the pork and sell it for you. Then you will not have to make the long trip into the village.'

'That would be a great help,' said his mother, 'if only I could be sure that you would sell it for the right price and not give it away to the first person who asks you for it. I will not take less than ten scudi (a scudo is an Italian coin which was then worth about five shillings) for it.'

'You can rely on me,' said Giufà, 'I will not sell it for less than that.'

He took the pork and set off for the village. On his

way there he met a man, who spoke to him politely and asked him what he had in the parcel he was carrying.

'A piece of pork,' said Giufà. 'I am taking it to market to sell.'

'How much do you want for it?' asked the man.

'Ten scudi. My mother will not take less.'

'A fair price,' said the man. 'I will buy it from you, and then you need not go all the way into the village.'

'Wonderful!' said Giufà, and he handed the piece of pork to the stranger.

'The only trouble is that I do not happen to have ten scudi with me just now,' said the latter. 'Never mind. I will give it to you tomorrow.'

'Very well,' Giufà agreed. 'Just tell me your name, so I will know how to find you.'

'I am myself,' said the stranger, and he went on his way, taking the pork with him. Giufà went home very pleased with himself. He told his mother he had sold the pork for ten scudi, just as she had told him to do.

'Where is the money?' she asked.

'The man who bought it did not have ten scudi with him, so he will pay me tomorrow. Don't worry. He is quite honest. He must be honest, because he told me his name, so that I could easily find him again.'

'What is his name?'

'Myself,' said Giufà proudly.

When she heard this the poor woman was really furious. 'Myself is only me,' she said. 'I mean, everyone is myself to themselves, just as you are myself to you.'

'I don't know what you are talking about,' said Giufà, who found this explanation much too difficult to follow. 'I will go and find Myself tomorrow, and then we will have the ten scudi.'

Next day he set off early in the morning, taking the same road towards the village. He stopped everyone he met along the way, asking them 'Are you Myself?', but no one answered him; they all thought he was quite crazy. Finally when he had asked at least a dozen people the same question, without receiving an answer, he said to one man:

'Well, if you are not Myself, who is? Where can I find him?'

The man shrugged his shoulders and, thinking to get rid of him, replied – 'How do I know? Myself might be anyone. He might even be that man over there, asleep on the edge of the road.'

'Do you really think so?' said Giufà, grateful for this advice. 'I will go and ask him.'

He went over to where the man was sleeping peacefully in the sun, and shook him by the shoulder. 'Who are you?' he asked. The poor man, still half asleep, said, 'Oh, go away and leave me alone. I am only myself.'

'Myself! Myself!' cried Giufà, overjoyed. 'At last I have found you. Now give me that ten scudi you owe me for the pork.'

'Pork? Ten scudi? What are you talking about?'

'You know perfectly well what I am talking about,' said Giufà indignantly, picking up a large stone from the side of the road. 'You owe me ten scudi. If you do not give it to me this very moment, I am going to drop this stone on your head.'

At this the sleeping stranger sat up. He looked at Giufà, who was as strong as he was stupid, he looked at the stone, and he looked up and down the road and saw that there was no one in sight just then in either direction. Completely bewildered, but seeing that there was no help for it, he took out ten scudi and gave them to Giufà.

'Thank you,' cried the boy, 'Thank you! I knew you were an honest man. I told my mother so. Now she will have to believe me.'

He went home again, leaving the unfortunate stranger to resume his nap. 'Here you are,' he cried to his mother; 'Here is the money for the meat.'

She took the money and counted it. 'Ten scudi. Who gave you this?'

'Myself!' said Giufà. 'Did I not tell you he was an honest man?'

Some time after this Giufà decided that he must find a job. So he went to work for an inn-keeper, in the village. The very first day he was there his master told him to take some tripe down to the seashore, and wash it there; it would be much cleaner that way than if he tried to wash it in fresh water. Giufà was delighted to be given such a task. The sun was shining, the day was warm, and he liked the sea.

He washed and washed and washed the tripe, until he was sure they were cleaner than any tripe had ever been before. Then he stood up and looked out to sea, across the Straits of Messina towards the coast of the Italian mainland, which was not very far away. A ship happened to be passing through the straits quite near to where he was standing. And Giufà was so pleased with himself, with his tripe, and with the sunny, summer day that he took out his handkerchief and waved to the ship.

It was not really his fault that the Captain of the ship, seeing what was apparently a white flag being waved on land, thought that someone must be in trouble and brought his ship into the shore. When the ship came to anchor, and the Captain stepped ashore, Giufà simply did not know what to say. In his embarrassment he held out his tripe, asking 'Do you think these tripe are clean enough?'

'What a rude way to greet a stranger!' The Captain, who now realized that he had made a mistake and that Giufà was only a silly boy who had been waving a handkerchief for fun, rebuked him. 'What do I care about your tripe?'

'Well, then, what should I have said?' asked Giufa, who was always ready to learn.

'Why, you should say something like, "May the Lord give you a good run,"' replied the Capain, who was thinking of his ship, and of the fair wind needed if he was to reach his destination that night.

'I see,' said Giufà, 'Thank you very much.'

The ship sailed on its way. Giufà took up his tripe and started back towards the village. On his way he passed a wood, where a hunter was in close pursuit of a deer; so near the deer, in fact, that he had his gun ready and was just about to fire. Thinking to be helpful, Giufà immediately called out 'May the Lord give you a good run!', whereupon the deer took to its heels so fast that the hunter had no hope of catching up with it again.

'You idiot!' he said, catching Giufà by the arm and shaking him roughly. 'Look what you have done. What do you mean by greeting anyone in that manner?'

'Well then, what should I have said?' asked Giufà.

'Why, you should say something like, "Lord, let them be killed!"' said the hunter, who was thinking of the game he had lost and how he would probably go home empty-handed that night.

'I see,' said Giufà. 'Thank you very much.'

He started on his way to the village again. Before long he met two men who were quarrelling fiercely about something or other, and had almost come to blows. Thinking he would be helpful, Giufà cried out loudly – 'Lord, let them be killed!'

'You idiot!' he said. 'Look what you have done.'

The two men stopped fighting and turned on Giufà. 'What on earth do you mean by that?' they demanded indignantly, almost in the same breath. 'What have you against us, that you wish us dead?'

'Nothing,' said Giufà. 'Nothing at all. I thought I was being polite. What should I have said?'

'Why, you should have said something like – "Lord, let them be separated!" ' said one of the two men, thinking of the best way to end a fight.

'I see,' said Giufà. 'Thank you very much.'

When he reached the outskirts of the village, he came to a church. There had just been a wedding in the church, and as Giufà passed by, the happy bride and bridegroom were standing on the church steps, surrounded by all their friends and relatives. Thinking that it would be polite to greet them, Giufà called out loudly – 'Lord, let them be separated!'

On hearing this, the poor bride and bridegroom clung to each other, crying 'Never, never,' while several of their friends ran down the steps to ask Giufà what he meant, and why he was so rude.

'Why, I only intended to wish them happiness,' said Giufa; 'What should I have said?'

'You should say something like – "Lord, make these people laugh," ' they told him, thinking of the wedding feast to come.

'I see,' said Giufà. 'Thank you very much.'

By this time he had nearly reached the inn. But as he turned down the street on which the inn stood he passed a funeral procession. The coffin, draped in black, was carried by eight mourners, and followed by a great number of other mourners, weeping. Giufà, crossing himself, stood back to let the procession pass, and as the coffin went by he called out – 'Lord, make these people laugh!'

The indignant mourners said nothing. But they all cast reproachful looks in his direction, scowling at him, and poor Giufà realized only too well that he had got it wrong again. 'Oh dear,' he said to himself, 'how will I ever learn the polite way of greeting strangers?'

To make matters worse he had taken so long to get back to the inn that it was now almost dark, and he had set off early in the morning. The innkeeper was waiting for him at the door.

'Give me those tripe,' he cried, giving Giufà a box on the ear, 'and be off with you. I never want to see you again.' He seized the tripe, went back into the inn and slammed the door behind him, muttering to himself as he did so, 'A whole day! One whole day to wash a bunch of tripe!'

So Giufà went home to his mother.

He did not find it easy to get another job; although he was willing to work hard, he really did not know how to do anything very well. As long as he had no job, he had no money to spend on clothes or on anything else for himself. But that did not stop him from buying clothes. He liked to be warm and comfortably dressed, especially now that winter was coming on, and he simply could not resist some of the clothes he saw in different shops, the knitted socks, the warm trousers, the leather jacket, the bright red beret. He bought all these, and more, promising to pay for them next day, or next week, or next month.

The days and weeks and months passed, and Giufà still had no money. The shopkeepers became more and more impatient, until he could scarcely ever walk along the village street without one of them stopping him and demanding indignantly when he was going to pay for the things he had bought. Poor Giufà could only say that he would pay all their bills in full just as soon as he had enough money. That was quite true. But it did not satisfy the shopkeepers.

Finally his creditors became really unpleasant and threatened to have him thrown into jail if he did not pay his bills. Giufà did not know what to do. It was all too much for him. 'I wish I were dead,' he thought to himself, and then he went on thinking – 'All right, I will be dead.'

He went into the village and bought one lily, promising the flower-seller that he really would pay for it very, very soon. Then he went home, lay down on his bed (still wearing the bright red beret, because he liked it too much to take it off), turned up his toes and crossed his hands on his chest, holding the lily. His mother came into the room before very long, saw him lying there, and, weeping bitterly, ran out to tell the neighbours that her poor son Giufà was dead.

The neighbours all came to mourn and to pay their respects. The inn-keeper and the flower-seller and the village shopkeepers came to sympathize with Giufà's mother, and one by one they knelt beside Giufà's bed, crossed themselves, and prayed for his soul.

'He bought two pairs of socks from me, and he never paid me for them,' said one shopkeeper. 'Never mind; I forgive him his debts.'

'I sold him that red beret,' said another, 'And he never paid me for it. Never mind. One must not speak ill of the dead.'

'I sold him the jacket he is wearing,' said a third shopkeeper, 'and he never paid me anything. It was a good jacket. Never mind; I forgive him.'

Giufà was delighted to hear these comments. He realized however that he had better not come back to life just yet. So he continued to lie there like a statue, not moving, scarcely breathing.

That afternoon the mourners came, placed Giufà's body in a coffin, and carried it through the streets to the church on the outskirts of the village. There, according to custom, the coffin would lie open until at least the following day; then the lid would be nailed down and the funeral services would take place.

Now in Italy a church is much more a part of the everyday life of the people than in some other countries. The Italians do not think of churches as places that one only enters once or twice a week, dressed in one's best clothes and speaking in whispers. They will go into a church in their ordinary working clothes, on their way to or from work. They may enter a church just to find a quiet place to have a nap, or to get away from the hot sun or the cold wind. Lovers may meet in church, where they will not be seen. In fact anyone who has a little time to spare, or needs a quiet place to get away from other people, is likely to go into a church; after all, they are beautifully decorated, with plenty of room, and they cost nothing.

So it was not quite as strange as it might seem to us that half a dozen robbers who were looking for a quiet spot where they could divide the spoils from their recent robberies should have chosen to enter the church where Giufà lay. They found an open space under the dome where there was enough light for them to see by, and there they spread out the gold and silver and jewels they were carrying. They divided these very carefully, their leader counting out – 'One for me, one for you, one for him, and for him, and for him,' until they had come to the end of the pile.

When they had finished there was just one gold coin left over. Then the robbers, although they already had so much that you would have thought they would have been satisfied, started quarrelling about who the last coin belonged to. They argued, their voices getting louder and louder, until at last the leader said:

'Look, there is a corpse in this coffin here. Let each of us fire a single shot with our pistols, and whichever of us comes nearest to the nose of the corpse shall have the gold coin.'

Giufà was not stupid enough to go on pretending to be dead when he heard this. He leapt to his feet and, standing up in the coffin, cried out in a loud voice:

'The time has come! Join me, my fellow dead men, and we will return to life again!'

The robbers did not wait to see what happened next. They dropped their pistols, dropped their gold and silver coins, and fled from the church in terror, falling over each other in their haste. Giufà waited until he was sure they were gone. Then he climbed out of the coffin, stuffed the gold and silver and jewels back into the sack in which the robbers had carried it, threw this over his shoulder and, whistling to himself, walked all the way home.

There was enough money in the sack for Giufà to pay the shopkeepers' bills in full, and buy himself as many new clothes as he needed. There was enough to buy his mother two sheep, and the flock of chickens she had been wanting for a long time. There was enough for all the food they could eat, and wine to drink, for many months to come. Giufà lived like a prince. But his mother wisely hid some of the money away for a rainy day. She knew her son well enough to know that sooner or later he would get into trouble again, and that then she would have to pay his bills for him.

And so, as they would say in Italy when they finished telling these tales – 'Now you must tell me your story, for mine are all told.'